Clint spotted Bogart immediately as the man stepped out of an alley across from Mills's office. They walked toward each other and stopped when they were close enough to hear each other without shouting.

"Adams."

"Bogart."

"That's right," Bogart said.

"The man who likes to beat women."

Bogart smiled at that, recognizing it as a ploy to try and upset him.

"You won't make me mad, Adams, and I won't get careless," he said. "I've been waiting for an opportunity like this for a long time."

"An opportunity to die?" the Gunsmith asked. "That's a hell of a thing to spend a lifetime waiting for."

Don't miss any of the lusty, hard-riding action in the Charter Western series, THE GUNSMITH:

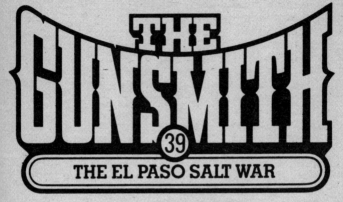

THE GUNSMITH

39

THE EL PASO SALT WAR

J.R. ROBERTS

CHARTER BOOKS, NEW YORK

THE GUNSMITH #39: THE EL PASO SALT WAR

A Charter Book/published by arrangement with
the author

PRINTING HISTORY
Charter Original/April 1985

ISBN: 0-441-30940-2

Charter Books are published by The Berkley Publishing Group,
200 Madison Avenue, New York, New York 10016.
PRINTED IN THE UNITED STATES OF AMERICA

To the Fast Draw League

ONE

El Paso, Texas—accessible to both Mexico and New Mexico—naturally boasted a large American and Mexican population, but was also home to many Germans, Canadians, and Italians. It was, however, the Anglos and Mexicans who fought for control. For instance, schools were a bone of contention between the two factions. Anglos wanted a so-called "free school" system while the Mexicans, led by the Catholic Church, wanted to retain a religious school system.

In El Paso the standard unit of commerce was not the American dollar, but the Mexican peso.

One hundred miles away, near Guadalupe Peak, lay the salt beds. Men were able to drive their wagons into the shallow lakes and shovel the salt onto the wooden floors. Water drained through the cracks in the boards, leaving behind dirty piles of salt. This was the favorite way for the border population to earn a few "coppers," which was a slang term for Mexican pennies.

Racism and greed quickly became a factor in the salt trade. Since the beds were on public land and free to anyone, there was a group of men who formed a syndicate called the El Paso Salt Ring to file a claim on the property and to charge a fee for every *fanega*—or two and a half bushels—of salt taken. Their attempts to monopolize the salt beds caused no end of harsh feelings among the workers in El Paso. It was into this explosive situation that the Gunsmith rode.

Clint Adams had made the ride northwest along the Rio Grande to El Paso a leisurely one. He needed the time to wind down from the events that had occurred in Eagle Pass between himself and King Fisher.*

He deserved a rest.

For a town that was hundreds of miles from most major ports of civilization, El Paso seemed to be a pretty lively place as Clint directed his rig down El Paso Street. Had he taken El Paso Street further past the town proper he would have ended up in Mexico, but he decided to stay on the American side.

After settling his rig, team, and Duke in the local livery, he went to the El Paso Hotel and

---

The Gunsmith #38: King of the Border

checked in, left his gear in his room, and headed for the nearest saloon, the Whiskey River.

Ben Williams was a member of the El Paso Republicans, one of the seven ringleaders of the El Paso Salt Ring. His partners were William Mills, Andrew Fountain, Judson Clark, Andre French, Samson Wager, and José Lujan. The fact that they were partners in making money, however, did not mean that they liked each other. And everyone in the Whiskey River Saloon that afternoon could hear it.

Clint was aware of the man at the bar who was grousing, first under his breath and then louder, but he was too busy making friends with a saloon girl named Mary Randall to care.

"I don't pay for my pleasure, Mary," he told her, "otherwise I'd take you right upstairs."

Mary was unlike the type of woman who usually appealed to the Gunsmith. For one thing, she was not even five feet tall, but it was her aura of tightly packed energy that attracted him. She had short, brown hair, a round face and powerful shoulders, and Adams just knew she would be like dynamite in bed. If he could get her there—for free.

"Well, Clint," she said, lacing the small fingers of her right hand with the long fingers of his left, "maybe something can be arranged."

"I'm glad to hear it," he said, but anything else he might have intended to say was drowned out by the shouts of the man at the bar.

"Goddamn them! Who do they think they are?" he demanded loudly. "They're all cheatin' me, you can bet on that. Especially that Fountain!"

"What's his problem?" Clint asked.

"Don't mind him," she said. "He just doesn't like his partners."

"Shouldn't be partners with anyone you don't like," he said, and then turned his attention back to the sexy little package sitting across from him.

A man hoping to get into the good graces of the El Paso Republicans entered Andy Fountain's office and informed him that Ben Williams was over in the Whiskey River bad-mouthing the partners in the Salt Ring, especially Fountain himself.

"By God, I've had enough of that big mouth!" Fountain declared. A man of advanced years, Fountain still backed down from no man. He picked up his walking stick and started for the saloon.

"I can take a break and then we can go upstairs," Mary told Clint. "Can we do what we have to do in a half-an-hour?"

"I hate to be rushed with something so pleasant," he said, taking her hand, "but I think we can do it."

"Well," she replied, "if we like it, maybe we can . . . do it again when we have more time?"

Clint just smiled and stood up.

Mary led Adams up the stairs to her room on the second floor. As soon as the door to her room closed, Mary rushed into his arms. He caught her and easily lifted her off her feet so he could kiss her. Her mouth was hungry for his, her tongue hot and searching. She moaned into his mouth as the kiss lengthened, and when it was broken, she was gasping for breath.

Clint turned neatly and deposited her on her bed. She got to her knees and began to take off her clothes. The Gunsmith followed suit.

When she was naked he was amazed, because she seemed even younger than her nineteen years than she had downstairs, though she was still very much a woman. What amazed him was the condition of her body. It was compact and powerful, her breasts were small and almost perfectly round, and her chunky, incredibly muscular thighs were getting him more excited by the moment. She reminded him of no other woman he'd ever been with.

She stood up on the bed, cocked her head for a moment and then said, "Did you hear shots?"

"Nothing that's happening downstairs could be as important as this," he told her, reaching for her.

She went willingly into his arms and as he buried his face between those firm breasts she moaned with desire.

"Williams!" Fountain shouted and immediately advanced on the man with his stick held high.

Williams was a younger, stronger man, but in his rage he immediately produced a derringer and fired as Fountain began beating him with his cane.

The first of the small caliber bullets hit Fountain in the left arm, which he was using to swing the stick, the second shot simply glanced off the top of his head; the third shot struck him squarely in the chest, penetrated a sheaf of letters he was carrying in his pocket, glanced off his pocket watch and broke a rib.

As Fountain staggered against the bar, Williams ran through the batwing doors out onto the street and towards his home, a few doors away.

Fountain stumbled from the saloon and ran headlong into his partners Clark and French. He told them what had transpired, then walked to his office as steadily as he could to get his rifle.

Clark and French started for the Williams residence. When they reached it, they found the door locked and began pounding on it, calling to Williams to come out. They were about to send someone for something they could use to break the door down when it opened abruptly, revealing Williams standing in the doorway with a shotgun held at his hip.

They separated as Williams fired at Clark, whom he liked no better than Fountain. Clark, a small man of middle age, ducked behind an adobe pillar. The first shotgun blast missed, so Williams took a step closer and the men proceeded to follow each other comically around the pillar until Clark finally stepped the wrong way. Williams squeezed off another blast, and Clark died instantly.

Fountain approached in time to witness this and wasted no time in taking aim and firing. Williams caught the bullet in the throat, twisted and fell to the ground. French rushed over, saw that Williams was still alive and drowning in his own blood, and mercifully fired a shot from his revolver into the dying man's head.

The El Paso Salt War was on.

TWO

Clint Adams and Mary Randall were totally oblivious to the violence that was going on outside. They were aware only of their all-consuming passion for each other. Clint was to find that Mary's enthusiasm *and* energy were virtually boundless.

Clint circled her pink nipples with his tongue for a short time before finally centering on those swelling buds. As he did so she spread her powerful thighs and then imprisoned the rock-hard length of him between them. While sucking on one nipple he slid his hands down over the line of her back to cup her wonderfully tight and smooth buttocks.

"Oh, Clint," she sighed, her legs beginning to shake.

"Lie down," he told her, and she obeyed immediately. Gently but firmly he turned her over so he could see her behind and began to cover those marvelously tight buns with kisses. Running his tongue down the crease between her cheeks, he reached between her thighs with his fingers and delved into the warm wetness he found there. Moving his tongue slowly toward her soaking slit, he removed his fingers and began to lick her lips.

"Oh, my God," she cried out as his tongue found her firm little nub. He fastened his teeth on it gently and began to circle it with his tongue. He felt it swell and then she started to ride up and down on his tongue as her body was wracked by spasms of indescribable pleasure.

"Do you need a rest?" he asked, peering up at her face from between her legs.

"God, no," she said. "We've only got about fifteen minutes left. Let's use them . . ."

She sat on his chest and then began to rub herself over him, working her way down until the head of his rigid cock was poking at her moist doorway.

"Ooh!" she exclaimed as she impaled herself on him, slamming her pubic bush against his. "Oh, yes!" she said, closing her eyes. She was actually squatting on him, jerking up and down and using those powerful legs to go faster and faster. He slid his hands up over her calves until he could feel the muscles in those incredible thighs as they worked beneath her skin, bringing her up and down on him, yanking a torrent of

10

hot liquid from him with long, deep strokes.

At this point Clint thought he could hear shots from outside, but that wasn't unusual in any town, and he certainly wasn't curious enough to stop what he was doing.

He gripped her buttocks tightly as he began to empty himself into her, lifting her so she could stretch her legs out and lie atop him, accepting all he had to give her.

"You're incredible," Clint told Mary as they dressed a few minutes later.

"Thanks," she said, looking almost shy at the praise, "but I think I'm also late."

"I'll come down and talk to your boss with you."

"No," she said, placing a restraining hand against his chest in what quickly became a caress. She brought her hand up to his face and said, "We can do this again tomorrow during the day . . . if you don't think me too wicked for suggesting it."

"I'd have considered you wicked if you hadn't."

He leaned down to kiss her open mouth, and then she pushed away from him. "I've got to go to work."

"I need a drink, anyway," he said. "You're almost too much for me to handle."

"Almost," she repeated, grinning.

11

They left the room and started down the steps together and noticed that something had obviously happened while they were away.

"I thought I heard shots," she said, reminding him. "I wonder what happened?"

"You go back to work so you don't get into trouble," Clint told her, "and I'll find out."

"All right," she said. "It'll give us an excuse to see each other tomorrow."

"As if we needed another one," he said, patting her behind as they reached the main floor.

"I live in a room above the café down the block," she whispered to him quickly.

"Good," he said. "We can kill two birds with one stone." When she frowned he added, "Breakfast and . . ."

Grinning she said, "I'm more interested in the 'and.' "

Clint had only to step outside and view the results of the violence that had taken place to reconstruct what had happened.

There were two dead men lying in the street, one with his midsection blown out by a shotgun blast, the other shot twice, once in the throat and once through the head. The second man was the man who had been complaining aloud in the saloon.

A third man was being led away by two others, and he was wounded.

There was a lawman standing around, looking

as if he wanted to talk to someone, but nobody wanted to talk to him. He was a short man, dressed in dark clothes with his sheriff's star pinned to the outside of his coat. None of the other men seemed to be paying attention to him, and when he spotted Clint nearby he approached with a comically stern look on his face.

"Excuse me," he said to the Gunsmith, "you're a stranger in town, right?"

"That's right."

"Maybe I can get an impartial explanation from you about what happened here."

"I wish I could help you, Sheriff," Clint said, "but I didn't see any of what happened."

"You didn't see anything?" the sheriff asked, obviously disappointed.

"I was in the saloon and heard this man complaining loudly about something," Clint said, pointing to the dead man who had been shot in the head, "but I didn't pay much attention to him since he was obviously drunk."

"Well," the sheriff said, "other people weren't as smart as you. I guess I better get over to the Doc's office and talk to Mr. Fountain."

"Mister" was said with a degree of respect, and Clint had another hint of how things stood in El Paso.

"Good luck," he said.

"Yeah," the lawman said sourly and hurried away.

Clint decided not to stay around and watch the cleanup activities that would soon take place. He forgot about his drink, and decided to go to his hotel and turn in for the night. If tonight was any indication, remaining in El Paso for a short while might prove interesting and pleasurable.

THREE

In the morning Clint decided to find the café that Mary had told him about, but to let her have her rest. He'd have breakfast first, and then knock on her door to see if she was . . . available.

He was on his way to the café, which was a few doors from the saloon in the opposite direction from where last night's action had taken place, when a buckboard skidded to a stop. A young woman leaped down, rushed up onto the boardwalk, ran into him and bounced off, falling on her behind.

"Why don't you watch where you're going?" she demanded angrily.

Clint, who had been in the act of bending over to help her up, stopped and said, "Excuse me, ma'am, but you ran into me."

"Damn it," she said heatedly. "Don't argue with me. Help me up."

She was in her early twenties, a tall, rangy girl without much meat on her bones, which was why she'd bounced right off of him. As he took her hand and hauled her to her feet it occurred to him that she was tall and thin, but weighed about the same as Mary. Her hair was long and dirty blonde, and she was wearing tight jeans and a man's shirt.

As she brushed off the seat of her pants, she said, "I'm in too much of a hurry to argue with you right now, Mr.—"

"Adams."

"Yeah, whatever," she said, shrugging off his name.

"What's your name?"

"My name is Fountain, if it's any of your business, and now if you'll excuse me—"

She bolted past him and went right through the doorway behind him. He checked the sign on the door and found that it was the doctor's office.

What name had the sheriff called the injured man by last night? Fountain, wasn't it?

He shrugged it off and continued on to the café.

In the doctor's office Sally Fountain asked the doctor how her father was.

"He's very lucky, Sally," Dr. Harvey said, patting her shoulder. He was not as tall as she, so he had to reach up to do it. "Williams fired three shots, and they all hit him, but it was a small-caliber derringer. One shot actually glanced off his skull, another hit him in the arm."

"And the third?"

"That's the one that did most of the damage, I'm afraid," the doctor said. "It gouged out his side and broke a rib."

"That's it?" Sally Fountain demanded, wanting to know the worst.

"As I said, he's very lucky."

"Can I take him home?"

"Home," the doctor emphasized, "not to his office. He has to rest. Your father is not a young man."

"I know that," Sally replied. "And believe it or not, so does he."

"You couldn't tell by his actions last night. He went after Williams with only his cane, and after he was shot went to get his rifle. He didn't get back in time to save Judson Clark, but he killed Williams with one shot."

"I'll take care of him. Where is he?"

"Inside. Help him get dressed, and he can leave."

As the young woman pushed past him and entered the other room, Dr. Harvey wondered what had turned what was once a sweet young girl into such a totally disagreeable young woman.

After a very satisfactory breakfast of bacon, eggs, biscuits and two pots of strong, black coffee, Clint found the doorway that led up to the second floor and ascended to Mary Randall's room.

He had knocked only once, and the door suddenly opened. Mary was standing there in a low-cut robe, with an infectious smile on her face.

"I thought you'd never get here."

"I figured you could use the rest," he said, grinning back. "You must have had a late night."

"Rest isn't what I need, Clint," she said, grabbing his right arm and pulling him into the room eagerly.

Slamming the door, she turned and leapt into his arms like a cannonball, knocking him onto her bed. Straddling his hips, she opened her robe and let it slide off, revealing herself to be totally naked, and smelling clean and fresh.

She pressed her pelvis tightly against his and felt him begin to swell. She unbuttoned his shirt and slid her hand over his chest and down to his belt, which she unbuckled. Quickly she undid his pants and slid her hands over his belly.

"We'll never get them off this way," he said, enjoying the weight of her tight, little body on top of him.

"I guess not," she said. She let him up and proceeded to get him into the same condition she was—naked. That done, she spread herself over him, pinning his rigid cock beneath her. Slowly she began to run her slick crack up and down the length of him, bringing him to throbbing readiness.

"Now," she said, rising up on her knees, but Clint grabbed her hips, lifted her up and dropped her on the bed beside him.

He climbed on top of her and said, "Now!" and drove the length of his hard cock deep inside her, bringing a sharp gasp of shock and pleasure from her.

He reached beneath her to cup her firm cheeks and she wrapped her powerful thighs around him. Holding her firmly in his hands, he dictated their pace, slow and long at first, then increasingly quicker. She loved the way his chest hairs rubbed her nipples, and he enjoyed the feel of her rounded belly against his.

"Oh, Lord—" she gasped against his neck. She rubbed her mouth back and forth over him, nipping at him with her sharp, white teeth. He moved his head so he could capture her mouth with his. She moaned loudly. Her lips and mouth were constantly in motion beneath his, sucking at him, chewing him and just generally enjoying him. He had never been with a woman who had enough energy to enjoy her unabashed need for sexual pleasure.

"Ooh, yes," she whispered against his mouth, bouncing her hips up and down so that it was all he could do to keep her bottom in his hands.

"Squeeze me, oh squeeze me hard, Clint. Please!" she cried out, and he closed his hands over her buttocks tightly, amazed again at how tight and firm she was.

As he was squeezing her as hard as she wanted, she was doing the same to him in more than one way. She had her strong legs and thighs wrapped around him so tightly that he thought she might stop his circulation, and her cunt had such a grip on him that he could have sworn she had a third hand deep inside of her, tugging insatiably on him. He felt longer than he ever had before, as if this little stick of dynamite was *stretching* him.

They were bouncing up and down so hard at one point that the bed was coming up off the floor and back down with such a thud he couldn't help but wonder what the people downstairs must be thinking. He forgot about them soon enough, however, when Mary ran her tiny hands up over his buttocks and pulled him even deeper into her steaming depths.

"Yes, yes, Clint, oh yes," she cried out, urging him on as she approached her peak.

"Oh Christ, oh Jesus," he grunted, as he pounded away relentlessly at her.

And finally she screamed as she came at the exact moment he began to fill her with a torrent of his scalding seed.

Not much later, with very little rest for either of them, she shinnied down to nuzzle his semi-erect penis with her nose, and then her tongue. Slowly, it began to swell and come to life for her.

"You don't need much rest, do you?" she said in admiration.

"Not with you, honey," he said honestly.

"Good," she said, covering the length of him

with one long lick, "because after this I still won't be done."

"Oh—" he started to say as she took the head of his cock into her mouth and swirled her tongue around it, and then took more . . . and more . . . until all of him filled her hot, wet mouth.

True to her word she was not done yet.

"I've got to be on top again," she said, huskily, "like last night . . ."

"Be my guest," Clint said obligingly.

She climbed astride him, squatted and took him into her to the hilt and began to ride him hard. He ran his hands over her thighs, once again enjoying the constant play of muscles beneath the surface as she milked him hungrily, her head thrown back rapturously, eyes closed, breath coming in labored gasps, lips drawn back in what could only be described as a gleeful smile . . . probably exactly like the one Clint was wearing himself.

Later, as Mary lay curled in his arms, they talked a bit about each other, telling some truths and, Clint had no doubt, some lies.

"I was born here, and I'll probably die here," she told him. "But in between, I'm going to have a good time."

"Why work in the saloon?" he asked. "It doesn't suit you at all."

"There's nothing else I can really do," she said. "I don't have any skills. Besides, it's not too

21

bad—and isn't that where I met you? Are you going to stay in town long?"

"Well," he said, honestly, "I hadn't intended to—"

She laughed and rolled over so that she was lying on top of him.

She licked his lips and said, "Did I have anything to do with changing your mind?"

"Only everything," he said, running his palms over her smoothly muscled buttocks.

"Good," she said, and reached down between them to take hold of him. "Maybe the longer I work on you, the longer you'll stay." When she smiled she did so with such joy that it showed in her eyes and radiated from her face.

"If I don't wear out first."

"How long would that take?" she asked playfully.

"I don't know," he said, "it's never happened before—but then I never met anyone like you before, Mary."

"Well," she said, spreading her thighs and then closing them, pinioning his cock between them, "why don't we try and see if we can find out."

FOUR

"Don't be treating me like I was some damned invalid," Andrew Fountain scolded his daughter as she assisted him into their house. They lived together on a small ranch north of town, but Fountain's "business" kept him in town so much that he was rarely there with Sally.

"As far as I'm concerned, you are an invalid," she snapped back. "You've got a broken rib, and you'll get into bed now."

"I'm damned if I will," he shot back. "There's going to be a meeting here tonight, and I won't have it take place at my bedside."

"A meeting?"

"Of the El Paso Salt Ring."

"You mean the El Paso Republicans."

The old man shrugged and said, "Same thing."

He turned to go to his den but did so too quickly and winced at the pain in his ribs.

"Do this, then," she said, attempting to strike

up a bargain. "Go to bed and rest until just before the meeting. I'll wake you in time."

He glared at her through bloodshot eyes and then relented. "Promise?" he said.

A rare look of tenderness passed over Sally's face and she said, "I promise, Pa."

"All right, then," he said, "I'll take you at your word, my girl—" and then as she moved to assist him, he added, "but for Christ's sake, I can get into bed myself."

"I'll have something ready for you to eat when you wake up," she said. Before he could protest she added quickly, "Don't worry. You'll be finished in plenty of time for your meeting."

He nodded and shuffled into his room.

Sadly, Sally Fountain couldn't help thinking that her father looked to her more and more like an old man. He was, of course. All she had to do was find some way to get him to admit it before he killed himself.

When Clint Adams and Mary Randall finally emerged from her room they went their separate ways. Another thing that Clint liked about her was that she hadn't started to act like they belonged together just because they'd been to bed.

"We're both out for the same thing, Clint—" she had said, "to enjoy ourselves. I don't expect anything else, and I hope you don't either."

Independent as well as beautiful, Clint had thought.

Mary went off to whatever errands or shopping she had to do, while Clint walked over to the sheriff's office. Last night he had met the sheriff of El Paso, but this morning he wanted to introduce himself formally, as he usually did when he arrived in a new town. He had found that letting the sheriff know that the Gunsmith was in town was usually appreciated. Most lawmen liked to be informed of potential trouble.

Of course, the sheriff had already had his share of trouble, judging from the incidents that had occurred the night before.

When he reached the sheriff's office he found a rather pretentious sign on the wall next to the door: WALTER J. BIEGELHEISEN, SHERIFF OF EL PASO. On the door was a sign that said WALK IN, so he did.

The little man who had accosted him the night before was seated behind a small, flimsy-looking wooden desk, clad in a dark gambler's suit. He did not, however, look any more like a gambler than he did a lawman.

"Sheriff," Clint said.

The sheriff looked up, frowned a moment as he tried to place Clint, and then said, "I talked to you last night, didn't I?"

"That's right."

Suddenly the man looked eager and said, "Did you remember something about last night that you want to tell me? Something important?"

"I'm sorry," Clint said, "but that's not why I'm here at all."

"Oh," the man said, looking dejected. "Well

then, why are you here? I'm very busy, you know."

"Being a stranger in town I just thought I'd come in and introduce myself to you, since I don't know how long I'll be here.

The lawman frowned again and said, "Why would you want to do that?"

Clint shrugged and said, "It's just a habit I've gotten into. Habits are hard to break."

"All right, then," Biegelheisen said, "go ahead and introduce yourself."

"My name's Clint Adams," Clint said and studied the man's face to see if there was any reaction.

There was not.

"Is that it?" the man asked with an expectant look on his face.

"That's it."

"Hell," the sheriff said, "I thought you were going to tell me you were Wild Bill Hickok, or somebody like that."

"No," Clint said, starting for the door, "nobody like that."

FIVE

Later that afternoon, the El Paso Salt Ring began to arrive at the ranch of Andrew Fountain. Sally Fountain saw Andre French, José Lujan, and William Mills into her father's den before going to his room to inform him of their arrival.

"Good," the old man said. He was sitting in his bed with his feet up—having just finished the dinner Sally had prepared for him—and now made a feeble attempt to bring his feet around.

"Damn it, girl, help me!" he snapped. Sally counted that as a small victory. If the old man recognized the fact that he needed help, maybe there was hope for him yet.

She helped him swing his feet around to the floor and put on his slippers.

"Are they all here?"

"Sam's not here yet."

"He will be," Fountain said, frowning with distaste. "He won't miss an opportunity to see you."

Sally did not bother to tell her father that, in

27

the past, Samson Wager had seen a lot more of her than the old man knew. In fact, Sam Wager was Sally's lover—that is, one of her lovers. Her father would also be surprised to discover that there were other members of the El Paso Republicans who had, at one time or another, been Sally Fountain's lovers.

She had already gone through Andre French and José Lujan, and was just about ready to try William Mills. Sally Fountain was in search of a perfect lover—*not* a husband. Sam Wager was getting boring, and Mills, though in his fifties, was a handsome figure of a man. Sally was only twenty-two but was seriously considering giving the older man a try.

"I'll go out and see if he's here yet," Sally said. "I will be out directly."

Sally went out to the den, saw that Wager was not yet there, and asked the men what she could get for them in the way of refreshments.

First French, and then Lujan, gave her knowing looks with their answers, and she wondered idly if either one knew that she had also slept with the other.

Did they talk about it? Compare notes?

She doubted it. These men—including her father—made very odd partners because there wasn't an honest drop of affection among them for one another. They didn't even associate with each other outside these meetings. Still, they made money by working together, and that was why they were partners. There had been seven, but with the deaths of Ben Williams and Jud Clark there were now five. Bringing the men their drinks—they all agreed to brandy—it occurred to her that she had never even considered going to bed with Ben Williams. He was a thoroughly disagreeable man—although she knew that the same had been said about her behind her back.

She didn't care. She cared little what the people in El Paso thought about her, especially the self-righteous, church-going women and wives. The only thing she cared about was that old man inside, with the broken rib and the hard head.

She heard a horse outside and went to the front door in time to see Sam Wager turn his horse over to a ranch hand. She stepped out to meet him on the porch.

"Sally," he said, rushing up the steps to hold her.

"Not here, Sam," she said, pushing his hands away.

"Why not?" he asked with a flash of anger. That was the only time Sam Wager was interesting, when he was angry. He was not a bad lover—better than French or Lujan, although that wasn't saying much—but he was a thoroughly boring man. "Don't tell me you're tired of me? You can't drop me like you did French and Lujan. I won't stand for it."

"What did you say?"

Wager laughed, leaned over, and kissed her quickly on the mouth.

"Sure, I know all about you and them—you and a lot of people, Sally. You're what's generally known as a whore."

Her right hand flashed towards his face, but he was quicker and caught it before it could make contact.

"Only you don't take money," he went on. "You do it for nothing."

She pulled her hand away from him and said, "You're wrong, Sam. I do it for enjoyment—and there isn't any more with you. In fact, there never really was."

Sam Wager was a big man, but he had never seemed potentially dangerous to her before. The look on his face scared her now though. He wasn't the same man she'd toyed with in bed; he was different now.

"Don't think you can treat me any way you want, Sally," he said in a low, even tone. "You can play with me as long as I let you—and I don't like it anymore." He grabbed her wrist and tightened his grip until she thought her bones would break. "I'm not like the other men you've toyed with, Sally. From now on we're going to play the game my way."

She was frightened, but she was angry as well, and she lashed out at him with the only weapon she had.

"Really, Sam?" she asked, trying not to let the pain show on her face. "How about your wife? Should we make her part of the game?"

His face changed and for a moment she thought he was the one who was afraid. At that moment the front door opened and Andrew Fountain looked out.

"There you are, Sam."

"I was just coming in, Andy," Wager said. He looked at Sally and said, "We'll finish our business later."

"I don't think so," Sally said.

As Samson Wager followed Andrew Fountain into the house, Sally wondered if she had picked the wrong man to fool with this time.

Then again, it might even be more interesting this way.

Sally wasn't allowed in the room while the El Paso Republicans/Salt Ring was meeting, so she took a walk around the grounds. Her thoughts moved from man to man, and dwelled briefly on what Sam Wager had called her.

Could you be a whore without taking money? What did it feel like, she wondered, to make love with a man for money? Could it really feel that different?

She started thinking about Williams Mills as a potential lover, and then abruptly abandoned the idea for two reasons. One, Mills wasn't married, and that could mean trouble after she got tired of him. The other reason was an odd one:

the man she had bumped into earlier that day. He was a stranger in town and she'd been too concerned about her father to give him a second thought until that moment. Nothing was stopping her now though, and the more she thought the more interested she became.

She decided to saddle her horse and ride into town.

SIX

Clint was playing poker in the Whiskey River Saloon when Sally Fountain came walking in, wearing faded jeans and a man's shirt that was too big for her. Still, when she walked in, the men in the room paid attention—and so did Clint.

"There she is," one of the men at the poker table said to another. "Fix your hair, Joe, maybe you'll be the one tonight."

"What does that mean?" Clint asked.

"That's Sally Fountain," the man said, jerking his head towards the bar. "There's more action going on between her legs than at ten poker tables."

"That's no way to talk about a lady," Clint said.

"She may be a lady," the man called Joe said, "but she don't act like one. That lady's been through half the men in this town—married or not—and she's probably getting ready to go through the other half."

"Is that so?" Clint asked, looking at the girl with interest.

"I call your raise, friend," Joe said to Clint. "What have you got?"

"Three Queens," Clint said, laying the cards out.

"Ah, shit," Joe said, throwing his two pair in.

Clint raked in his money and said, "You boys will have to excuse me."

"Where you going?" Joe asked. "Ain't you gonna give us a chance to—"

"Another time," Clint said, walking toward the bar.

"Where's he going?" Joe asked the other man as Clint got up from the table.

"He's gonna try his luck in a new game, Joe," the other man said. "Stop bellyachin' and deal. Now that he's gone, somebody else can win."

Clint examined the tall girl critically as she undressed and climbed into his bed. She had to be almost six feet tall. Sally had hardly any breasts at all, but she had large, brown nipples. Her legs were long and slim, yet shapely, as were her almost boyish buttocks; between her legs was a thick tangle of dark-blonde hair. Even though her ribs showed, this girl had a special appeal that she probably took advantage of—if what the men at the poker table had been saying was true.

"What did they tell you about me?" she asked, watching anxiously as he undressed.

"Who?"

"The men you were playing cards with."

He told her exactly what they had said, word for word, and she threw her head back and laughed.

"You find that funny?"

"Come here," she said, extending her arms to him, "and we'll talk after."

He got on the bed next to her, barely touching her, and leaned over to run his tongue around her large nipples. She shivered and moaned at the first touch, and her eyes seemed to go out of focus as she pushed her hand down between her own legs.

"Don't do that," he whispered, pulling her hand away.

"What?" she asked, momentarily confused.

"Don't touch yourself," he said. "I'll give you all the touching you need."

She stared at him a moment and immediately realized that she would not be able to toy with this man or control him in bed. He was going to do what he wanted to do.

This might be the one, she thought, as his hand slid down over her belly. This just might be the one.

Clint felt his hand get lost in her pubic bush as he wrapped the hair around his fingers. He began to chew in earnest on her right nipple, and she dug her hands into his hair. He slid a finger through her thick patch and sank it into what felt like a warm bog. She was already soaking wet.

"Oh, God . . ." she moaned as he moved his finger around inside of her and began chewing on the left nipple.

She closed her legs hard over his hand. Trapped there like that, he did the only thing he could do—sank another two fingers into her and found her clit with his thumb.

"Oh, Lord . . ." she cried out as he continued to stimulate her above and below the waist.

"Your tongue," she said, "oh please, I want your tongue—"

Using his tongue he probed through her wet hair and finally tasted her. Finding her slippery cleft, he delved into it and swirled his tongue around. Her hips came up off the bed to meet the pressure of his tongue as if someone had hit her in the stomach.

He put his hands on her bony hips, pinned her thighs to the bed with his elbows, and then slowly slid his tongue up to her swollen clit, flicking at it tentatively.

"Oh Christ, Clint, Christ . . ." she moaned, "what are you doing!"

"Just relax."

"I can't," she complained, trying to move her hips but finding herself hopelessly pinned. "You've got to let me move."

"No, I don't," he said, swooping down on her clit with his mouth.

When his tongue hit it, she screamed and tried

even harder to move, but he held her fast and began to suck on her.

"Oh, Jesus, you bastard, you lovely, lovely bastard . . . yes, that's it . . . Christ, stop . . . no, stop . . . don't . . . ever . . . stop!"

He had no intention of stopping—or even of slowing down—at least not until he had wrung every spasm of pleasure from her that he possibly could.

"Oooh . . . Ohh . . . Oh shit, do it, suck it, bite it," she cried out. "Oh, Clint, I want you, please . . . you've got to . . . to . . . Ahhh!"

Her flat belly began to tremble and suddenly it was as if she exploded inside. Quickly he mounted her and slid his throbbing cock deep inside of her and began to pound himself into her as hard and fast as he could. When she opened her mouth to cry out he covered it with his own so that her cries of pleasure were muffled. He knew she'd be able to taste herself on his mouth, and wondered how she would react. Surprisingly, she pulled her mouth away from his and began to lick his face, as if seeking to get all of her own juices off of him. Then, as he felt that great rush that started in his legs, he covered her mouth again. When he shot his hot seed into her, she screamed right into his mouth, raking his back with her nails and kicking his buttocks with her heels.

SEVEN

"Gentlemen," Andrew Fountain said, addressing his partners, "I know that we are not all that fond of each other, but we do make money together, do we not?"

"Nobody's ever argued that, Andy," Sam Wager said. He was still annoyed at Sally Fountain and wondering how he could keep her under control without having her threaten him with his wife. Sally was amazing in bed. She did things to him—and wanted him to do to her—that his wife, Judith, would never—

"I'm concerned, Sam," Fountain said, breaking into Wager's thoughts, "that what happened last night might start a trend."

"You're the one who killed Ben Williams," Andre French pointed out.

"After he killed Jud Clark."

"He got killed trying to bring him in for shooting you, which wouldn't have happened if you hadn't gone after Ben in the saloon with your stick!" Sam Wager said.

Wager was the only man present who was a member of the Salt Ring, but not the Republicans. At 35, he was the youngest man present, and possibly the most ambitious. Right now his primary ambition was to replace Andrew Fountain as leader of the Salt Ring. Fountain's loss of control, which had caused the deaths of two of their members, was his best chance to date to do so.

"Andy, you have to admit, you shouldn't have gone after Ben that way. All he was doing was talking, for Christ's sake."

"He's got a point, Andy," José Lujan said.

"Ben's no loss," William Mills pointed out, coming to Fountain's defense—as Wager had expected.

"That's not the point," Wager said. "This has damaged our operations, and our reputation."

"Reputation?" Mills said. "The people in this town hate us."

"And we don't have to give them any more reason to do so," Sam Wager said. "I don't know about anyone else here, but I've got ambitions of going further in politics than El Paso."

"We all know of your ambitions, Sam," Andrew Fountain said wearily. His wounds were

40

beginning to bother him, and he wished Sally were there to help him back to bed. He'd be damned if he'd ask any of the men present to do so—except, perhaps, for Mills.

"All right," Mills said. "I think we're all agreed that we'll have to watch ourselves from here on in."

"Especially Andy," Sam Wager said.

"I won't lose control again!" Fountain snapped, and then grimaced.

"Let's leave and let Andy rest," Mills suggested, noticing the pain on his friend's face. "He's been through a lot, whatever the reason."

"Agreed," Sam Wager said, standing up. "I hope you feel better, Andy."

"Thank you," Fountain said, knowing that Wager didn't mean a word of it.

As the men rose to leave Fountain said, "Will, stay for one more drink."

"You need your rest, Andy. Sally'd have my head—"

"Will!" Fountain said tightly.

"All right," Mills sighed, "one more."

"See the others out, will you?"

Mills accompanied the others to the front door and was disappointed when he didn't see Sally around. She wouldn't be interested in an old goat like him anyway, he thought.

"Are they gone?" Fountain asked when Mills returned.

41

"Yes, they're gone."

"Christ," Fountain said, doubling over, "get me to bed, Will!"

EIGHT

"Now we talk?" Clint asked.

"I . . . don't know if I can . . . yet," she said, breathlessly.

Sally Fountain had never experienced anything like it before, and now she was confused. She had finally found her perfect lover, but what was she to do with him now?

"Maybe," she said, rolling towards him and lowering her head, "we should just—" her words stopped as she took his semi-erect penis into her mouth hungrily.

Clint hesitated for a moment, then pulled her head up. "Now we talk," he said firmly, and she nodded breathlessly.

"You want to know why," she said, finally catching her breath.

"Why what?"

"Why I've been to bed with so many men, and

why I don't care how many people know about it."

"All right," he said, "why? I assume you're father is fairly wealthy."

"He is."

"Why would a girl with that kind of money act like a—"

"A whore? You can say it. Someone else called me that tonight. I don't care about what people think. I enjoy sex, but I haven't yet found a man who could match my enjoyment—up to now, that is."

"Is that what you've been looking for?" he asked. "A man who enjoys it as much as you do?"

"Yes," she said. "A man who isn't afraid to do whatever he wants, and whatever I want—and now I've found you."

"What does that mean?" he asked. "I mean, now that your search has ended."

She looked pensive for a moment and then said, "Well, I don't have any illusions about marriage, that's for sure."

"Thank God for that."

She stuck out her tongue at him.

"You'll be leaving soon, so I guess I'll just have to get as much of you as I can before you do—that is, if you want to see more of me."

"I can't see any more of you than I have tonight, that's for sure," he said, giving her an exaggerated once over.

She looked at him carefully and said, "Have

you found another girl in town already?"

He considered lying to her, but figured why bother and answered, "Guilty."

"Who?"

Somehow he didn't think he should give that information out just now.

"Sally—"

"I told you I don't have any illusions about marriage, Clint. I also don't feel that I own you now just because we made love."

"Why do you want to know who the other woman is then?" he asked.

"I told you, I like a man who's not afraid to try anything," she said, "and I'm not afraid to try something new. After you licked me you kissed me. That was the first time I had ever tasted . . . myself. Do other women taste like that?"

He thought he knew what she was getting at.

"All women taste different."

"Really? Do you think your other lady friend would want to . . . join us?"

He stared at her.

"Do I shock you?"

"No," he said, seriously, "I was just thinking over your question."

"You mean you're interested?"

Damned if he wasn't, he thought. He could only remember having been with two women at one time once before, and that had been a mother and daughter, so they had each concentrated on him. To be with two women who might not concentrate solely on him. . . . Well, that was intriguing.

"I'll ask her."

Clint asked Sally if she was going to stay the night and she shook her head negatively.

"I've got to get back to the ranch and look after my father. His meeting should be over by now."

"What kind of meeting?"

She smiled serenely and got up from the bed.

"I don't talk about my father's business dealings," she said, picking up her clothes from the floor.

He watched her get dressed, amazed at how attractive she was even though she was so damn skinny. What was it about her?

"What kind of business?"

She shook her head and sat down on the bed to pull on her boots.

"Did it have anything to do with what happened last night?"

"I'll tell you what caused last night," she said, standing up and stamping her feet to get a better fit from her boots. "That old man is stubborn. He won't admit that it's time to stay on the ranch and rest."

"Convince him," Clint said. "You seem to be a pretty persuasive lady."

"Ha!" she said. "Not with that old man." She turned to look at him and said, "I have to go."

"Don't let me stop you."

"You probably could." She leaned over and

kissed him warmly. "Thanks."

"For what?"

"For this evening—and for not judging me."

"I'm the last person to judge anyone."

"Why?"

He smiled the way she had smiled when he asked about her father and shook his head.

"Not talking, huh?"

"We'll talk again."

She walked to the door, opened it, and said, "I guess we'll be seeing each other."

"I guess."

"A couple of real independent souls, huh?" she said, smiling.

"That's the only way to be."

"Let me know what your other girl friend says," she said, and left, closing the door gently behind her.

He laid back in bed and clasped his hands behind his head, studying the ceiling thoughtfully.

What would she say, he wondered.

NINE

When Sally arrived back at the ranch she found everyone gone but William Mills.

"Will," she said by way of greeting. "Where's my father?"

"In bed. He was in pain, and I had to help him." She started for her father's room, but Mills stopped her. "I think he's asleep."

She looked in on him anyway and found that he was indeed asleep, apparently resting peacefully.

Returning to the den she said to Mills, "Thank you for staying with him, Will."

"He was asking for you."

"I was . . . busy," she said evasively, although she knew she wasn't fooling him.

"He shouldn't get out of bed, Sally."

"I know that," she said, with a touch of annoyance.

Mills moved closer to her and put a shaking

hand on her shoulder. She affected him like no other woman ever had, yet he was sure she never gave him a second thought.

"If you need any help with him, Sally, please call on me—for anything."

She gave him a puzzled look and then said, "Thank you, Will. I'll remember."

"I'll see myself out."

As he left she had the feeling that her father's friend might be interested in her as a woman. If she wanted to, she knew she could have him. She probably could have seduced him right there in the sitting room if she'd wanted to.

She was no longer thinking in those terms however.

She went to the kitchen, took a chair from around the table, carried it into her father's room, and sat down by his bed, prepared to spend the night there.

Sally was there the next morning when Fountain woke up. She offered him a choice of breakfast.

"Just coffee," he said.

"You've got to eat something, Pa," she tried to argue, but he would have none of it.

"Just get me the coffee, girl, and then sit with me. We have to talk."

She went and made him some coffee. In an effort to get some kind of food into him, she broke an egg into it. When he sipped it, he either did not taste it or chose not to mention it, because he drank it down.

"What do we have to talk about, Pa?" Sally said.

"Death."

"But Doc said you were gonna be all right."

"Yeah," Fountain said, "this time. What about next time?"

"What do you mean, next time?"

"Sally, I think the others are going to try to kill me."

"Others?"

"Don't be dense girl!" he scolded. "The Salt Ring, the Republicans."

"But who? Why?"

"One of the others," Fountain said. "I think he wants it all for himself."

"Which one?"

"That I don't know, but whoever he is, he got Ben all heated up the other night and pushed him into doing what he did—and I didn't help matters any."

"Pa—"

"Hush, girl. I was a damn fool doing what I did. I played right into the hands of whoever's planning this."

"Do you suspect anyone?"

"I wouldn't put it past any of them."

"Including Will Mills?"

Fountain frowned. "I'd hate to think that, but—"

"What about Sam Wager?" Sally asked, remembering how different Sam had seemed last night. Maybe he had been that way because his plan was underway, and he'd already gotten rid of Williams and Clark.

"I guess he would be the one to suspect, all right," Fountain said. "He's young and strong-willed." Fountain suddenly looked his daughter right in the eye and said, "Don't you get involved with him, girl."

"With Sam?"

"I've seen the way he looks at you. I'm not as blind as you think I am," he added. She suddenly wondered if he knew more than he was saying.

"What do you want to do, Pa? Leave?"

"Leave hell!" he snapped, grimacing again. "I was here when this town started. I ain't about to leave now."

"Then what?"

He thought a moment, then said, "I don't know. I guess the smart thing to do would be to hire me a gun."

"A bodyguard?"

"I guess, but I'm talking about a gunfighter, somebody like Warren Murphy or Clint Adams."

"Clint Adams?" she asked, surprised. "Why him?"

"Well, hell girl, he's only the fastest gun around now that Hickok's dead. 'The Gunsmith' they call him. If I could get him, Sam Wager or whoever's up to no good would think twice before trying to kill me."

"The Gunsmith," Sally whispered. She'd heard the name before, but she hadn't known that his real name was Clint Adams.

"I have to go to town, Pa," she said, springing up from her chair.

"Well, leave the coffee here, then," he commanded as she reached for the pot.

"Will you be all right?"

"I ain't helpless!"

"I'll be back as soon as I can."

"Sure you will," he said, skeptically. As she was going out the door, she heard him shout, "And don't think you were fooling anybody with that egg in my coffee!"

TEN

When Clint woke the next morning he decided over breakfast that if he was going to stay in El Paso for any extended period of time—and Lord knew that either Mary or Sally alone was a good enough reason—he was going to have to do one of two things: either send a telegram for some money or drum up some work.

If he sent a telegram for money it would either have to go to Rick Hartman in Labyrinth, Texas, where he had a bank account, or to Brightwater, Arizona, where he had a piece of a saloon run by Buckskin Frank Leslie. He decided that instead of bothering either one of those gentlemen he'd just go out and do some honest work.

Before leaving the café he let the owner know that he was a gunsmith, and if anyone needed

any work done they could find him at the livery
stable. He passed the word at a few more places,
and then went to the livery to open his rig for
business.

That was where Sally Fountain found him later
that morning, hard at work trying to work some
magic on some pretty badly abused guns.

"Clint!" she cried out.

"Hello, Sally," he said, peering out at her from
inside his rig.

"I've been looking for you everywhere!"

"Well, I've been here. What's wrong?"

"Should I come in or will you come out? I want
to ask you something."

He put down the gun he was working on and
stepped outside.

"What is it?" he asked, seeing that she was
flushed and out of breath.

Now that she had his attention, however, she
didn't seem to know how to put her thoughts into
words.

"Sally, if you want to ask me something, just ask
me," he said, trying to make it easier for her.

"Um—is it true that you're the Gunsmith? I
mean, the famous Gunsmith?"

He grimaced and said, "Yeah, I guess it's true.
Why?"

"I want to hire you."

"Hire me? Do you have a gun that needs fixing,
Sally, because that's the only kind of work I hire
out for."

"No, I don't want you to fix a gun," she said, quickly, "I want to hire *your* gun."

Clint stiffened and said, "My gun is not for hire, Sally."

"But I thought—" she began, puzzled.

"I know. That's what everyone thinks." He took a deep breath to calm himself and then said, "I guess I can't really blame you though."

"Oh, Clint, I wasn't trying to insult you," she said desperately. "I'm just worried about my father."

"All right," he said, taking her by the shoulders. "Why don't we both just calm down, and you can tell me what the problem is."

They sat on the bottom step of his rig.

"You know what happened to my father the other night."

"He was shot, and he killed a man."

"My father thinks that one of his partners riled Ben Williams into doing what he did, hoping that something like that would happen."

"Why would someone do that?"

Sally gave Clint a quick rundown on the Salt Ring and the Republicans. "Pa thinks that someone is out to get everything for himself. Will you help us?"

"I'll help," Clint said with a smile, "but not for money."

"For what, then?" she asked with a frown.

He reached for her, pulled her close and kissed her warmly and deeply.

"For future considerations," he said. "Let's go and see your father."

From a window overlooking the street a man watched as Clint Adams and Sally Fountain rode down El Paso Street towards the end of town, obviously heading for Andrew Fountain's ranch. He watched them until they disappeared from sight and then turned to face the man who was seated on the other side of his desk, Ray Bogart.

Bogart was a tall, lanky man in his late thirties. His clothes bore recent trail dust, and in point of fact, his horse was tied off behind the building, still panting from the ride to El Paso in reply to a telegram telling him that there was "work" for him there. He had not yet been to the hotel or the livery.

"I'm glad you came right here, Bogart," the man said.

Bogart regarded the man coolly and said, "You said you had work for me. If I don't like it, there ain't no sense in my paying livery or hotel expenses. I'll just mount up and be on my way."

"You'll like it," the other man said, seating himself behind his desk. "It's right in your area of expertise."

Ray Bogart's "area of expertise" was killing people. He did it well, enjoyed it, and had a reputation for success.

The man behind the desk noticed that when

the gunman sat he did so solely on his left buttock, leaving the gun on his right hip accessible in case the need should arise suddenly. He could see where Bogart had gotten his reputation for competence.

"All right, I'm here," Bogart said. "What's the job?"

"I want you to kill someone."

Bogart's thin slash of a mouth jerked minutely to the left. "Tell me something I don't already know."

"I want it understood, however, that it will be done at a time of my choosing."

"And the place?"

"Of your choosing."

"And the price?"

"In keeping with the caliber of man you are to face."

"And who might that be?"

"Clint Adams."

Bogart did not show any outward reaction.

"The Gunsmith," the other man said.

"I know who he is," Bogart said slowly.

"Will you take the job?"

Bogart's eyes bored into the other man's for a moment as he ran the palm of his right hand up and down his thigh.

"Oh yeah," Bogart said, eyes glittering. "I'll take the job, all right."

When Ray Bogart had named his price his

potential employer had balked momentarily, until Bogart had risen to leave, then he had given in.

Bogart left by the rear entrance, took the reins of his horse and walked him to the livery without stopping at the saloon for his usual bottle of whiskey. Once he had put his horse up, he registered at the hotel, and had a bottle sent up to his hotel room.

Like any professional gunman he'd heard the stories about the Gunsmith. The man was a legend, but Bogart had a lot of confidence in himself, in spite of the impressive list of gunmen that the Gunsmith had put out of business: Kid Dragon, Dale Leighton, and John Stud just to name a few. Bogart had seen Stud's move and thought he could have taken him. He'd heard talk that Adams was friendly with Warren Murphy, the Irish Gun, another man with a big reputation. Bogart had never seen Murphy's move nor the Gunsmith's for that matter.

But he'd remedy that real soon.

When the man in the office had sent for Ray Bogart, he had not even known that Clint Adams was in the area, and even after the Gunsmith showed up, there was a chance that he would not get involved with Salt Ring business. But when he had seen Adams and Sally together, he knew his instincts were right. Sally had probably already been to bed with him—which made him seethe with anger—and now she was taking him out to the ranch to stand guard over her father, that useless old man who stood in the way of everything he wanted.

Everything that Ray Bogart was going to help him get by the power of his gun.

ELEVEN

When they reached the Fountain ranch, Clint was a little surprised at its appearance. Apparently Andrew Fountain was more businessman than rancher, and the general condition of his ranch showed it.

"It's not much of a ranch anymore," Sally said, reading Clint's expression. "My mother never wanted Pa to get involved in business and town politics. But when she died, it was what he used to keep going. It kept him sane after her death, and it's all he's known since. It tears him up inside that he's not gotten beyond El Paso."

They relinquished their horses to a ranch hand and Clint followed Sally into the house.

"Pa, you in bed?" she called out.

"Where the hell else would I be?" Clint heard the old man bellow back.

"Sounds like he's feeling better," Clint commented.

63

"He's always like that. Come on."

Clint followed her into her father's bedroom. The man on the bed appeared to be extremely frail.

"Who is this?" the old man asked.

"This is a friend of mine, Pa," Sally said, sitting by her father's bedside. "His name is Clint Adams."

The old man's eyebrows went up, and he looked from his daughter to Clint a few times before he said, "The Gunsmith."

Clint grimaced, and Sally said, "That's right."

"How long have you known the Gunsmith?"

"We met the day your daughter picked you up from the doctor's office, Mr. Fountain," Clint answered for her. "We . . . bumped into each other."

"I bumped into him," Sally clarified.

"And now you're friends?"

"A stranger in town tends to make one or two friends pretty quickly, Mr. Fountain. Just to make it a little less lonely."

"I see," Fountain said, looking from one to the other again. "Why are you here?"

"I asked him to come."

"Your daughter tells me you're having some trouble. She thought maybe I could help."

"For how much?"

"Pa!"

"It's a fair question, Sally," Clint said, defending the old man's right to ask it. "For nothing, Mr. Fountain."

The old man gave him a look of pure disbelief—and scorn.

"The Gunsmith? Hiring his gun out for nothing?"

"I didn't say anything about hiring my gun out, Mr. Fountain," Clint said. "I don't hire my gun out."

"Sure. That's how you got your reputation."

"How I got my reputation is not important, Fountain," Clint retorted. "I'm offering my help to keep you alive until you can decide what you want to do about this mess you're in."

"What mess?"

"That's not my place to say."

"No," Fountain said, "if you're gonna be working for me—whether I pay you or not—I want to hear your opinion."

Clint looked at Sally and she nodded.

"Based on what I know, which isn't a hell of a lot, I think it's time for you to retire. If you're in someone's way enough for them to want to kill you, then for God's sake get the hell out of their way."

"That's your opinion?" the old man demanded.

"That's it."

"And what's yours?" Fountain asked Sally.

She regarded her father sadly and said, "I

think he's right, Pa. If it's Wager, or Mills, or whoever it is, get out of his way. Let him have what he wants and stay alive."

Fountain looked at Clint then and said, "I accept your offer of help, Mr. Gunsmith—"

Sally heaved a sigh of relief, but caught it when her father continued.

"—but not your suggestion. I would appreciate it if you would stay around long enough for me to get back on my feet, and I'd prefer that you watch over Sally more than me."

"Why me?" Sally said.

Fountain looked at Sally and tenderness invaded his face.

"If they want to get at me bad enough, honey, they might do it through you."

Sally looked at Clint. "He's got a point, Sally," Clint said.

"Thank you," Fountain said. "I wouldn't mind if you collected your gear from the hotel, Mr. Adams, and moved in here—temporarily."

Clint looked at the feisty old man and said, "Of course."

Sally rode back to town with Clint and waited in the lobby while he collected his gear. While she was waiting Sam Wager suddenly entered the lobby and walked up to her directly.

"Hello, Sally."

Wager suddenly seemed a much more imposing figure than he had ever before, and she actu-

ally backed away from him a step before reply-
ing.

"Sam. What are you doing here?"

"I happened to be passing by and saw you
coming into the hotel. We have some unfinished
business."

"No, Sam," Sally said. "All of our business is
finished."

"Not until I say it is, Sally."

"No, Sam."

Wager grabbed Sally's elbow hard. "Don't say
no to me, Sally."

"Why?" Sally retorted. "Hasn't your wife ever
said no to you?"

"My wife—" Wager started to say, tightening
his grip even more, when he spotted Clint coming down the steps.

"Is something wrong?" Clint asked. He had his
saddlebags over his left shoulder, and was holding his rifle in his left hand.

"Nothing to concern you," Sam said.

"I don't think I know you," Clint said.

"Sam Wager, not that it's any of your business,"
Sam said.

"Would you mind taking your hand off her
elbow, Mr. Wager?"

"This is between Sally and me."

Clint looked at Sally and asked, "Is it?"

"No," she said, trying to pull free of Wager's
grip. "We have no business at all."

"You heard the lady," Clint said.

Wager tried to match stares with Clint Adams, but couldn't. He released Sally's arm and said to her, "Another time."

"What about me?" Clint asked.

Wager simply stared at him, then turned and left the hotel.

"Who was that?" Clint asked Sally as they left the hotel moments later.

"He was . . . " Sally admitted, after a second of hesitation. "He's also a member of the El Paso Salt Ring."

"That's right," Clint said. "You and your father mentioned his name earlier, didn't you?"

"Yes."

"You both feel that he might be the one?"

"He's the youngest, and the most ambitious of my father's partners."

"You'll have to tell me about him," Clint suggested, "and the others."

"There's something I can tell you about Sam Wager right now, Clint," she said as he tied his saddlebags to Duke's broad back and slid his rifle into its leather sheath.

"What?"

"He's a dangerous man, Clint."

When everything was secure Clint patted Duke's neck and turned to face Sally.

"Maybe in his arena, Sally," he said to her, "but not in mine."

TWELVE

Back at the ranch Sally made lunch for Clint and her father. After serving her father in bed, she sat with Clint in the kitchen and told him about her father's partners.

"Clark and Williams are dead," Clint told her before she got started, "so there's no use in discussing them. Tell me about the rest."

"Andre French owns the bank in El Paso," Sally said.

"Has he ever . . . *lost* any of the bank's money?"

"If he has, he's found it before anyone could notice."

"All right, what about the others?"

José Lujan, she told him, had a successful ranch in the area, although he wasn't very successful at anything else that he did.

William Mills, her father's oldest friend, was a

lawyer and handled many of the big ranchers in the area, including Lujan and Fountain.

"And Sam Wager?"

"Sam owns the Whiskey River Saloon."

"He's a little out of place with the others, isn't he?"

"He's ambitious, and the others seem to like that. I think they all feel that Wager can do them some good, but Sam is only out to do himself good."

"They think they're using him, and he's actually using them."

"Right."

"Now, tell me who you're using."

"What?"

"How many of these men have you slept with?"

He watched her face as she tried to decide whether or not to become angry.

"How well do you think you know me?" she finally asked.

"I don't know you as well as I'd like to, but it didn't take me very long to discover how aggressive you are, did it?"

"No, it didn't," she said. "All right, I've slept with Andre French, José Lujan, and Sam Wager."

"Wager being the most recent."

"Yes."

He stared at her for a few moments, then said, "I'm not going to ask you why you've slept with these men—"

"Boredom, mostly," she answered, without giving him a chance to finish.

"It's none of my business," he said, "but I wanted to know because I plan to visit all of these men and have a little talk with them."

"About what?"

"About your father. I'm simply going to suggest that it wouldn't be wise for anyone to try to harm your father while I'm staying in this house."

"But Sam—"

"Sam Wager," Clint said, standing up, "is the first man I intend to visit. How serious is he about you?"

"I don't know," she said, honestly. "He's married, but it was fairly easy for me to . . . get him interested."

"I don't wonder. Is it over now?"

"As far as I'm concerned it is," she said. "He never struck me as the type of man who'd want to hold on, but suddenly he's changed."

"Or maybe you never knew the real Sam Wager," Clint suggested. "Maybe he was playing with you instead of the other way around."

"Be careful of him, Clint."

"I'm always careful, Sally. What should I know about the others?"

"Nothing," she said. "They're all businessmen who at one time or another had a hankering to be in politics."

"What about the Salt Ring? Was that formed

with any political basis?"

"No. Only to make money."

"Would the others do their own killing, or hire it to be done?" he asked.

"It would be hard for me to imagine them doing either," she replied. "But I guess they'd hire it out."

"All right," he said, starting for the door. "I'll be back soon."

"Do you think it's safe for you to leave?" she asked, walking him to the front door..

"I don't think anyone will try anything in the daylight. I'll be back to spend the night."

"Can I count on that?"

Clint grinned, nodded his head slowly and said, "See what I mean—aggressive."

The first person Clint saw when he entered the Whiskey River Saloon was Mary Randall. She crossed the room to meet him at the bar.

"You haven't been around," she said, smiling. "I've been getting lonely."

"Not you."

"Lonely for you," she clarified. "Do you have time to go upstairs?"

She was so pretty, this small, young woman who vibrated with energy.

"I have to see the boss," Clint said, "but if you happen to be in your room when I finish . . ."

She grinned broadly, as infectious a grin as he had ever seen, and said, "Don't even knock."

"Where's Wager's office?"

"Straight back," she said, pointing.

"Thanks."

Clint walked past her to the door of Wager's office and entered without knocking.

"Wha—" Wager said, looking up from his desk with a frown. When he saw Clint he stood up and demanded, "What the hell do you want?"

"I think we should have a talk."

"I don't have anything to talk to you about," Wager said loudly.

"I think you do."

"If this is about Sally Fountain—"

"It's not," Clint said, cutting him off, "it's about Andrew Fountain."

"Andy?" Wager said, frowning again. "What about him? Is he all right?"

"He's fine, and I intend to keep it that way."

"What does that mean? Did he hire you to be his bodyguard? Is that old man starting to—"

"He didn't hire me," Clint said, again cutting Wager short, which the other man did not like at all. "Let's just say I'm going to be his house guest until Mr. Fountain is feeling better, and I'd hate for anyone to try to make sure that he doesn't."

"House guest? You're staying at the Fountain ranch?"

"That's right."

"In the house?"

"Right again."

"With Sally?"

"She lives there, doesn't she?"

"I won't have it!" Wager said, slamming his hand down on the desk top.

"You have nothing to say about it. Besides, I thought you didn't want to discuss her."

"I don't. I'll just tell you that she's mine."

"That's not the way she sees it."

"She'll come around."

"And what about your wife? Will she come around?"

"I don't want to discuss my wife with you either, Adams," Wager said tightly. "I think it's time for you to leave my office."

"I've had my say," Clint replied. "Just remember what I said about Fountain."

"Get out."

Clint left the office and started for the batwing doors before he remembered Mary. One look around the room told him that she wasn't working, which meant she was waiting for him upstairs. He thought briefly about her thighs, and then changed direction and headed up the stairs.

Her door was not locked, and when he entered he found her waiting for him on the bed, invitingly naked. When she saw him she rose to her knees on the bed.

"I was starting to worry."

"About me?"

"That you weren't coming."

"How could I stay away?"

He approached the bed, and she changed position so that she was seated on the mattress. He sat on the bed and gently pushed her down so that she was lying on her back, and then he leaned over her and started nibbling the nipples of her small, taut breasts.

She busied herself with his clothing, pulling his shirt off and running her hands over his chest. He abandoned her breasts long enough to disrobe completely. As he joined her on the bed she reached for the rigid column of flesh between his legs and started to stroke it.

"I can't wait," she said, and he could tell by her quivering lips that she was more than ready.

She pulled his cock down until the head was pushing at her wet opening, and then suddenly he was sliding inside of her.

"Yes!" she said, wrapping those powerful thighs around him. He began to move in and out of her while she kissed his neck, face, and mouth eagerly. When her time came she thrust her tongue deep into his mouth, moaning so hard that his teeth vibrated. He sucked on her tongue so it seemed that while he was fucking her with his penis, she was doing it to him with her tongue.

When he erupted inside of her, she pulled her mouth loose so she could moan out loud, and her insides milked him of every hot drop.

THIRTEEN

After Clint left Mary, he made his way over to the bank to talk to Andre French.

The first thing Clint noticed when he was led into French's office by an assistant was that there was nothing French about the man at all. If anything, French looked Irish, with a full, red face and broad shoulders.

"Mr. French?"

"That's right. What can I do for you, friend? You want to open an account?"

"My name is Clint Adams," Clint said, "I'm a friend of Sally and Andrew Fountain."

"Sally *and* Andrew?" French asked, looking dubious. He obviously thought that Clint was another of Sally's conquests.

"That's right."

French shrugged and said, "What's that got to do with me? When my assistant said you wanted to see me, I assumed you wanted to open an account."

"I'm sorry to disappoint you," Clint said. "All I really came to tell you was that I'll be a guest of the Fountains out at their ranch until Andrew gets back on his feet."

"Is that so? And why would I be interested in knowing that?" French asked, his Irish accent showing now.

"Well, you're his partner, aren't you? I figured you'd be interested to know that he'd be safe at home."

"Safe from what?"

"From anything," Clint said, "and from anybody. That's all I've got to say, Mr. French."

With that Clint turned on his heels and left French's office, wondering what had brought an Irishman to El Paso, Texas, and caused him to change his name to, of all things, Andre French.

The Gunsmith's next stop was the office of WILLIAM MILLS, ATTORNEY-AT-LAW, as the sign on his office door read. His office was in a one-room above the town hall. Clint knocked on the door and entered as a man's voice called out for him to do so.

Mills was seated behind his desk as Clint entered and showed no inclination to rise. He was a man in his fifties with broad, heavy shoulders and a barrel chest. His hair was gray and thinning on top. He sat with his chubby, square-fingered hands folded on the desk in front of him.

"Can I help you?"

It took only that many words for Clint to surmise that Mills was drunk, or well on his way to becoming drunk.

"Mr. Mills, my name is Clint Adams."

"So?"

"I'm a friend of the Fountains."

The man laughed and said, "You mean a friend of Sally, don't you?"

"And her father."

"That young minx," Mills said, as if he hadn't heard Clint. "She's screwed every man in this town except me, and now she's taking up with strangers."

Mills's tone was bitter, and Clint realized that the man was obviously either in love with Sally or simply wanted her very badly.

"Mr. Mills, I've only come here to tell you that I'll be a guest at the Fountain ranch until Mr. Fountain is fully recovered from his wounds."

"Sleeping in Sally's bed, are you?" Mills demanded, his face becoming red. Clint noticed that the man was making an effort to keep his hands folded on the desk top.

"I'm afraid that where I'll be sleeping is none of your business, Mills," Clint said. "All you need to know is that I'll be out there, watching over Mr. Fountain."

"Watching over?" Mills said, shaking his head and frowning, as if trying to understand. "You mean, Andy's hired you to be his bodyguard?"

79

"I'm not getting paid, Mr. Mills, but I guess you could say I was a bodyguard."

"Against whom?"

"I'm sure, Mr. Mills," Clint said, moving towards the door, "that either you or one of your partners would know the answer to that question better than I."

After leaving Mills's office Clint retrieved Duke from in front of the Whiskey River Saloon and rode out of town to José Lujan's ranch, following Sally's directions.

Lujan's ranch was larger and certainly better maintained than Andrew Fountain's place. Clint was greeted at the front gate by a *vaquero* who accompanied him to the main house and made him wait while he asked Mr. Lujan if he wanted to speak to him.

Lujan appeared with the cowboy and instructed the man to care for his guest's horse.

"I won't be here that long."

"Oh, but surely, Señor, you will join me for a drink. I have some very fine brandy."

"You talked me into it."

Clint followed Lujan into the house. The Mexican was only about five foot nine, but he appeared to be in excellent physical condition for a man in his mid-forties. His dark hair was slicked down and shiny, and his mustache was very small but well-manicured.

"Please," Lujan said, stepping aside so that Clint could precede him into a large den.

"I recognized your name immediately, Señor," Lujan said, pouring two glasses of brandy from an expensive crystal decanter. He turned, handed one crystal glass to Clint and said, "You are the one they call the Gunsmith, no?"

"That's right," Clint said, tasting the brandy and finding that it was indeed excellent.

"To what do I owe the honor of such a visit then? Are you here looking for employment, perhaps? I could use a man of your talents, and I would pay you well."

"I'm afraid not, Señor Lujan. I have just visited all of your partners in the Salt Ring, and I will tell you the same thing I've told them."

"Which is?"

"I'll be staying at the Fountain ranch until Mr. Fountain has full recovered."

"You are their guest, then, and not an employee?"

"That's right."

"I see. Well, thank you very much for telling me this."

"Don't you want to know why I'm staying?"

"Well, obviously Andrew is not well, and Sally . . . well, Sally is Sally, is she not?" Lujan laid a friendly hand on Clint's left arm and said, "I am sure you have your reasons, my friend."

Lujan was impressive. Clint gave the man his empty glass, declining another drink. Lujan walked to the front door and called for his horse to be brought around.

"Perhaps you will have time for a longer visit while you are here, amigo. I would look forward to that."

"It's a possibility," Clint said, mounting up.

"Be comfortable, my friend," Lujan called out as he rode away. "I am sure Sally will do her best to see that you are."

FOURTEEN

"Did you see them?" Sally asked anxiously when Clint had returned. She didn't even wait for him to dismount, but came running out of the house as soon as he rode up.

"Let me take care of Duke, and then we'll talk."

"I'll come with you."

She followed him to the stable. While he un-saddled Duke, he heard her rummaging around, doing something with the hay, and then he heard her lock the doors.

"What are you up to?" he asked. As he turned to face her she was taking off her jeans, having already removed her blouse and boots.

"Now that you've taken care of Duke," she said, putting her hands on her slim hips, "you can take care of me. *Then* we'll talk."

"Sally—"

"It has to be out here, Clint," she reasoned.

"We can't do anything in the house with my father around."

She had a point there. Just recently having "taken care of" Mary, this was going to be a severe test of his stamina.

She came forward, took his hands and led him to the bed she had made out of hay. Releasing his hands she laid down on her back and then beckoned to him. Clint felt himself responding to Sally, who was panting like a bitch in heat.

Joining her on the hay bed, he ran his left hand through the tangle of hair between her legs, finding her slickly moist, and as he pushed two fingers into her he began to nibble her large nipples. While she was lying on her back, her breasts flattened out to the point where they almost disappeared.

"Ooh," she moaned as he wiggled his fingers deep into her bog. Her hands came up to cup the back of his head as he continued to work on her dark-brown nipples.

"Oh God, Clint, I want your mouth on me, I want your tongue inside of me—"

He knew how much she enjoyed it when he used his tongue, so he slid down between her slim thighs and set to work on her, using his lips and teeth as well.

"Ooh, yes, that's it, right there, lick it. Oh, God! Suck it," she cried, wrapping her fingers in his hair and pushing his face against her crotch.

He fastened his lips on her rigid little nub and,

while sucking, flicked it back and forth with his tongue until he finally drove her over the edge.

"Oh, yeahhh . . ." she moaned as she came. Then Clint climbed up so that the tip of his swollen cock was just touching the sensitive lips of her cunt. She reached around, grabbed his buttocks and pulled him into her.

He began to drive himself into her, not giving her time to come down from her previous orgasm. Suddenly she was bouncing up and down on the hay bed in the throes of a second one, imploring him to do it harder, banging her pelvis into his with all her might.

"Now we'll talk," he said, feeling as if they had played this scene before. He stood up and began to dress while she lounged naked on the bed of hay.

"What happened?" she asked.

"Nothing much," he said, buckling his gunbelt. "I simply visited each of the partners and told them that I'd be a guest out here until your father was back on his feet."

"That must have thrilled them all, especially Sam Wager," she said.

"It did. Lujan was very polite, Mills was a little drunk when I spoke to him, and French was rude. He's the first Irishman I ever met with a French name."

"He tries to hide the fact that he's from dirt poor, Irish farm people."

J.R. ROBERTS

"He doesn't do a very good job."

"How did Sam Wager react?"

"He told me to stay away from you, going so far as to say that you were his."

"Hah! I don't belong to any man."

"You like rolling in the hay too much," he said, grinning at her.

"Look who's talking," she said, grinning back, putting her hands behind her head so that her small breasts thrust forward impudently. "Tell me you didn't visit your "friend" while you were in town."

"I did," he said honestly.

"It didn't seem to affect your performance any."

"Thank you."

"By the way, did you talk to her about what we discussed the other night?"

He'd forgotten all about that. "I haven't had time."

"Well," she said, "maybe when this is all over, before you leave town."

"Maybe," he agreed. "Aren't you going to get dressed?"

"When we're done."

"When we're done? I'm dressed!"

Getting up on her knees she grabbed his belt buckle and said, "That wasn't my idea!"

86

FIFTEEN

Ray Bogart was in the Whiskey River Saloon, admiring Mary Randall's energetic body when he got word that his employer wanted to see him.

He went to the man's office and sat down across the desk from him.

"This better be good," Bogart said, "I was sizing up something sweet over at the saloon."

His employer peered at Bogart intently before he realized what the man meant.

"Have sex on your own time."

"That was my time. All my time is my time until you cut me loose on Adams."

"It was someone else I had in mind," the man answered.

"Well, good. I'd hate to get out of practice."

"I want you to go out to the Fountain ranch."

"Where is it?"

"I'll get to that," his employer replied. "I want you to go out there and kill someone."

"Who?"

"Anyone but Clint Adams—"

"He's out there?"

"Stop interrupting me!"

"Go ahead and finish," Bogart said with an amused expression on his face. He realized that his employer was more than a little drunk at that moment.

"Kill anyone but Adams and the two people who live there, Sally and Andrew Fountain." Briefly, the man described the two Fountains to Bogart.

"Seems to me I heard something at the saloon about a man named Fountain getting shot up a few nights ago."

"And he'll get a lot worse before the week's out," the other man replied, "but not tonight. Tonight one of his people gets killed. Now, you will have another man with you—"

"No," Bogart interrupted, shaking his head emphatically. "I work alone."

"I said you will have another man with you who will think that he is getting paid to help you," Bogart's employer explained. "That man is not to return with you—do I make myself clear?"

"He's part of the job?"

"Exactly."

"Is that it?"

"No, that is not it. You will also leave the man's horse behind. Is that clear?"

"It's clear."

Bogart didn't bother asking why. It was none of his business, even though it wasn't very hard to figure that his employer was looking to blame something on somebody else. Leaving a branded horse behind was one way to do it, but leaving a dead man behind to be identified was another. Doing both just about made it clear-cut. Bogart wondered if Clint Adams was dumb enough to go for such a setup. He doubted it.

"Is that it?"

"That's it," the man behind the desk said. "Get it done and then come and see me tomorrow. I'll pay you for the men you've killed."

Bogart grinned and said, "That's just what I like to hear."

"Where are you going now?"

"Back to the saloon," Bogart said. "There's a little gal there who's gonna get real lucky."

"When will you do it?"

"After dark, when I get the feelin'."

"The feeling?"

"Mister, I got to have the feelin' before I kill someone, and this little gal is gonna help me get it."

When Bogart left, his employer was slumped behind his desk, hoping he hadn't made a mistake hiring Bogart. But he needed someone to do the dirty work. Williams was the only one of the partners who could have been pushed to violence—him and Andy Fountain, but the old man was past that now.

It was going to have to be up to him to do all the pushing now—through Ray Bogart.

Ray Bogart was beginning to get that feeling.

He had each hand full of a smooth, muscular buttock while he drove his rigid organ between them, enjoying the tightness of the saloon girl's little brown hole. She was moaning and groaning as he continued to poke into her until suddenly he was spurting his hot juice into her, getting the feeling that there wasn't anything in the world that could stop him from doing what he wanted to do.

Ray Bogart was definitely going to get that feeling tonight.

SIXTEEN

"Is he settled in?" Clint asked Sally.

"He's asleep, already," she said, sitting next to him on the sofa, which was to be his bed.

"This coffee is great," he said. She had made it strong and black, the way he'd said he liked it.

When she didn't respond to the compliment, he looked at her and saw that her mind was evidently far away.

"What's wrong?"

"Oh!" she said, startled. "I'm sorry, I was just thinking."

"I could see that, but about what?"

"My father. I'm worried about him. A few years ago—hell, even last year—he would have bounced back from something like this quickly."

"And now he's not bouncing back?"

"Not at all. In fact, I think he's getting worse.

He didn't want to get out of bed at all today. That's not like him, Clint."

"Maybe you should have the doctor come out and look at him tomorrow."

"I think you're right." She looked at his empty cup. "Are you finished?"

"Yes. Let me help—"

"No, no, you sit there, and I'll clean up. Then I'll make up your bed," she said, and he detected regret in her tone. He too regretted the fact that he'd have to sleep on the couch alone while she was just a few feet away in her own bed.

He had been lying on the couch for about a half-an-hour, clad only in his long underwear when he heard a door open and the padding of bare feet on the floor. It was the bare feet that told him it was Sally.

"Clint," she whispered.

"Hmm?"

"Are you asleep?"

"No."

"Good."

He was able to make out her silhouette as she knelt next to him and placed her hand over his crotch, unbutoning the flap. She had most of his cock in her mouth when they heard the shot, and she bit him painfully by mistake.

"Sorry, Clint. What was that?"

He was already holding his gun and moving

toward the door, ignoring the pain in his prick.

There was a full moon and the clearing between the house and barn was fully lit, but empty. He stepped off the porch just as the second shot sounded and saw the flash of light in the bushes between the barn and the bunkhouse. He ducked, not knowing if the shot was meant for him, and fired twice at the flash.

"Clint?" Sally called from behind him.

"Stay in the house!" he shouted and ran toward the bushes.

As he approached, he heard the sound of a running horse moving away from him. He broke through the bushes and tripped over the prone figure of a man.

The bush cut off the moonlight there so he bent over to peer closely at the man.

"Clint!" Sally called, coming through the bushes. She had gotten dressed.

"I told you to stay in the house."

"One of our men is dead."

"That first shot?"

"Must have been," she replied. "The others say he heard a noise and said he was going out to have a look. Next thing they know they heard a shot and Jim was on the ground, dead."

"This man is dead, too. Is he one of yours?"

She bent over to take a look and then said, "No."

"Then he was one of them. He was shot in the

back of the head. From the way he fell, I'd say he was facing the house when he was shot."

"You mean his own partner shot him?"

"That's how it looks."

"That doesn't make sense."

"His horse might be around here," Clint said. "Have a couple of your men look around, and if they find it, bring it to the barn."

"Right."

Clint stared down at the dead man, who probably had no warning or inkling of what was in store for him when he came out here.

The question now was: Why?

The dead man and his horse were brought into the barn.

"All right," Clint said, "does anybody recognize him?"

Aside from the dead hand the Fountains had four others working for them, and all four stepped forward to examine the man. While they were at it, Clint moved next to the horse to check its brand.

"What's the Cross-J?" he asked, looking at the "J" with a slash through it.

"Slash-J?" Sally asked.

"I suppose."

"That's José Lujan's brand," she said.

"Is that right?"

"Hey," one of the hands called out, "now I recognize him, Miss Fountain."

"From where?" Clint asked the hand, a jug-eared, freckle-faced man in his early forties. Clint couldn't help wondering if Sally's search for the perfect lover had taken her into her own bunkhouse.

"He works on the Lujan spread," the hand answered.

"Lujan again," Clint said.

"Do you think José sent them here to try and kill my father?" Sally asked.

"After I told him I would be here?" Clint asked. "He'd have to be a fool to do it tonight."

"José's no fool."

"Well, somebody thinks I am," Clint said.

"Why?"

"They sent some men out here—probably two—to shoot one of your men at random. Then one of them killed this man and left him and his horse behind to implicate Lujan."

"Then José isn't the one."

"Not necessarily."

"But you just said—"

"Lujan struck me as a clever man," Clint said. "He could have set this whole thing up to make himself appear to be in the clear."

"Then we're back where we started."

"Except that we've got a dead hand, and another body on our hands. I think we ought to send someone for the sheriff."

"Biegelheisen?" she asked. "He won't do anything. He used to be the town dentist before he was appointed sheriff."

"Who appointed him?"

"The town council."

"And who sits on the town council?"

Sally gave him an ironic smirk and said, "Guess."

"The El Paso Salt Ring/Republicans."

"Right."

"We need him anyway, just to stay legal." Clint turned to the jug-eared man and said, "Would you mount up and go into town for him, and the undertaker?"

"Sure, if that's what Miss Fountain wants me to do."

"I'd appreciate it, Hank," Sally said.

"Sure, ma'am," the man said. Clint could have sworn he saw him blush before going to saddle his horse.

"The rest of you can go back to bed, boys," Sally said, and the other three men left the barn, talking amongst themselves.

"More conquests?" Clint asked her in a low voice.

"They wish."

"Let's go and wait in the house," Clint said, aware of a throbbing in his penis. "I've got something for you to take care of."

Sheriff Biegelheisen arrived with the undertaker over an hour later. By that time Sally had "examined" Clint's penis, and satisfied to find it still in good working order, helped him get dressed.

"Glad you could make it, Sheriff."

"It's my job to make it," the little man said, dropping down off his horse. "Where's the body?"

"In the barn. There are two bodies."

"I'll be the judge of that," the lawman said, as if he hadn't heard a word Clint had said.

"Hank, would you show the sheriff . . ." Sally said, and the jug-eared man led the way.

"I told you," Sally said to Clint.

"You've got to stay on the side of the law in this, Sally," Clint said. "If that means dealing with Biegelheisen, then that's what you'll have to do."

"If you say so."

Hank and Clint helped the sheriff and the undertaker load the two bodies onto the undertaker's rig. Then the sheriff approached Sally with such a serious expression on his face that it was almost humorous.

"Miss Fountain, I'm sorry your night's sleep had to be disturbed," the little sheriff said gravely.

"That's very kind of you . . . Sheriff," Sally said, trying her best not to laugh at the man.

"In the morning I'll go see Mr. Lujan about this," the lawman continued. "This invasion of your privacy will not go uninvestigated."

"There's a lot more here than just invasion of privacy, Sheriff," Clint said.

"I'll be the judge of that," the sheriff said, then tipped his hat to Sally and mounted up to follow the undertaker's rig back to town.

"The doctor," Clint said to Sally.

"Oh, yeah," she replied, and then called out, "Oh, Sheriff!"

"Yes, ma'am?"

"Could you do me a favor and ask the doctor to come and check on my father tomorrow?"

"It would be my pleasure, ma'am," Biegelheisen said, touching his hat again. He wheeled his horse around and rode off into the dark after the undertaker.

As he rode away, Clint rubbed his jaw and cast a questioning eye towards Sally, who read his mind perfectly.

"Jesus," she said, "not even in his wildest dreams!"

"You owe me for two bodies," Ray Bogart told his employer.

"It's done?"

"I wouldn't be here if it wasn't," Bogart said.

"Were there any problems?"

"Everything went smoothly," Bogart answered. "All that's left is for you to pay up."

He watched the man walk to his desk, open the top drawer and take out a brown envelope.

"It's all there," the man said, handing it to Bogart.

Bogart took it and stuffed it into his pocket.

"Aren't you going to count it?"

"I trust you."

"That's not good business."

"It wouldn't be good business on your part to cheat me," Ray Bogart said, heading for the door. "It also wouldn't be very healthy."

"Where will you be if I need you?"

"Check the hotel, or the saloon. I'll be at one or the other—waiting."

SEVENTEEN

Doc Harvey came out early the following morning and was met by both Sally and Clint on the front porch.

"I heard you had some excitement here last night?" he said, stepping down from his buggy.

"Quite a bit," Clint said.

"How did your father react?" Harvey asked, speaking directly to Sally Fountain.

"He didn't," Sally said. It had worried her the night before that her father had not even awakened to the commotion, and she mentioned this now to the doctor.

"I'll check on him then," Harvey said, taking his black bag from the buggy. "Is he awake?"

"Yes."

"Has he had his breakfast?"

"He doesn't want any."

"Well, you make him something while I'm in with him," he instructed her. "He's got to eat."

"All right."

Clint stayed in the parlor drinking coffee while the doctor went into Andrew Fountain's room and Sally went into the kitchen. He was still there when Harvey came back out, shaking his head, but refrained from asking any questions about the old man's condition.

Sally came out of the kitchen now and said, "Doc?"

The doctor put down his black bag, picked up an empty cup and poured himself a cup of coffee without asking.

"I don't understand it," he said finally. "Your father has always been a fighter, Sally."

"And now?"

"His injuries are healing, but the problem is not there," the doctor went on, as if he were speaking to himself. "The problem is in his head."

"Doctor, could you explain that to us?" Clint asked.

Harvey turned and looked at Clint, then moved his gaze to Sally before speaking.

"He doesn't want to get out of that bed," he told her, "and he's convincing himself that his injuries are keeping him there."

"And they're not?"

"Oh, he'll hurt like hell if he tries to get up, but I never knew that to stop Andy Fountain."

"I never did either."

"Has he talked to you, Sally?"

"We've talked some."

"Well, talk some more. He's got to want to get well, or he just won't."

"Is he in danger of dying?"

"He's an old man, Sally," Harvey said, putting his coffee cup down. "If he doesn't eat and keep up his strength, yes, he could die—but it would be by choice."

"That's not his choice to make!" Sally said fervently, and although Clint felt differently he did not openly argue with her.

"Tell him," Harvey said, picking up his bag, "not me."

As he started for the door Sally called out, "What do I owe you, Doc?" but he just waved his hand behind him and continued walking until he was in his rig and gone.

Sally looked at Clint and said, "I've got to make him eat some breakfast."

"You go ahead. I've got to go out for a while."

"Where?"

"I think I'll visit Señor Lujan and have some more of that excellent brandy of his."

"If you're going to stay there for any length of time, watch out for his sister."

"I didn't know he had a sister."

"Believe me," she said, "if you're there more than fifteen minutes, she'll make sure you know."

"What does she look like?"

"You'll find out," Sally said, turned on her heel, and stormed into the kitchen.

Apparently Sally Fountain did not have warm feelings towards José Lujan's sister.

That made him curious about meeting her.

Once again Clint presented himself to the *vaquero* at the gate of the Lujan spread. The man was not the same man who had been there last time, but the procedure was the same. Clint followed the man to the clearing in front of the house, and waited while he was announced.

"My friend!" Lujan called out as he came out the door. He turned and said something in Spanish to his man, who descended the steps and took Duke's reins. "How nice that you have returned so soon."

"I couldn't ignore such a gracious invitation to come back," Clint said.

"But of course you couldn't." Lujan beckoned for Clint to ascend the steps and enter his house. "Come in, come in. We will have a drink and talk."

When they were installed in Lujan's den, each with a glass of brandy, Clint came right to the point.

"I have a reason for coming, Señor Lujan."

"Of course you have, my friend," Lujan said. "Please, have a seat and tell me what it is."

"Has the sheriff been here yet?"

"Our funny little sheriff?" Lujan asked, laughing. "No, he has not. Why? Should I expect him?"

"I think you should."

Lujan frowned mightily in jest and said, "Should I be very worried about this visit?"

"Not if you're innocent."

"Of what?"

"Of sending one of your men to the Fountain ranch last night to try to kill Andrew Fountain."

Now when Lujan frowned it was the real thing. He studied Clint carefully.

"I do not understand."

"Are you missing a man?"

Lujan put his glass down and left the room. Clint heard the front door open and heard Lujan shout something in Spanish, and then the door closed behind him, cutting off the sound of any reply. As he started to look away his peripheral vision picked up a movement out in the hall. As he turned his head to take a better look, he caught a brief glimpse of a shapely form with long, black hair, dressed in riding clothes. Before he could investigate, he heard the front door and a short exchange of Spanish. Then it shut once more, and José Lujan reappeared.

"Yes, one of my men left last night and has not returned. Do you know where he is?"

"I imagine he's at the undertaker's."

"You killed him?" Lujan asked after a moment of hesitation.

"It was supposed to look that way."

"I do not understand."

Clint told the Mexican rancher what had happened the previous night, and what his theories were about the incident—all his theories.

"Do you think me such a devious man that I would have one of my men killed to give the illusion of innocence?"

"I think you could be very devious, yes."

"Perhaps, but never that devious, my friend. My men trust me; that is why I command their respect." With a hurt look on his face Lujan added, "I would never do such a thing."

Clint studied the man for a moment. "Damn, if I don't believe you."

"Well, thank you for that. Now the question is, who did do such a thing?"

"That's what I have to find out, Señor Lujan," Clint said, "and I won't do it sitting here drinking your excellent brandy."

Lujan rose and walked Clint to the front door.

"If I can be of any help, Señor Adams, please do not hesitate to call on me," he said while Clint was climbing up onto Duke's massive back.

"Thank you, Señor Lujan."

"I feel that you must also call me José," Lujan said. "I would be honored if I were allowed to call you my friend."

Although Clint believed the man's denials, he still didn't know if he was ready to trust him completely.

EIGHTEEN

He was out of sight of the house, but still on Lujan's land, when he became aware that someone was following him.

"Easy, Duke boy," Clint said, directing the big black horse up a grassy knoll to a stand of trees. "We're getting some unexpected company."

They waited patiently, until they were able to hear the sound of a horse approaching.

"Here they come, big boy."

As the rider passed the trees he and Duke were hidden behind, Clint kicked Duke into action, and the big horse exploded beneath him. They came down out of the trees like a shot, and Clint saw the rider ahead of him, dressed in riding clothes, long black hair streaming behind—her.

Duke caught up to the woman's horse in a few strides and Clint reached over and grabbed the reins, then looked at the rider and caught his breath.

She had dark skin, dark eyes and eyebrows, flaring nostrils and a wide, full mouth.

"Miss Lujan, I presume?"

"Let go of my horse," she said, tossing her head haughtily.

"Not until you tell me why you were following me."

"I was not!"

"Yes, you were."

"I was simply riding on my brother's land, as I often do," she said. Her Spanish accent, not heavy but still noticeable, added to her allure—not that her physical appeal needed any help. "You do not belong on this land."

"You saw me in your brother's house, so you know I was his guest. I'm simply riding back to town."

"Town," she said, "is the other way."

"Is that right? I must have gotten lost," he said, releasing the reins on her pinto.

"I doubt that," she said, studying him with obvious interest.

"I tell you what, Miss Lujan—"

"Carmen."

"Why don't we stop playing games and talk straight to each other."

"Very well," she said, smiling, "we will—how you say—talk straight."

"And your English is damn good, so let's not have any of that 'how you say' act."

She laughed aloud now and said, "As you wish, Señor Adams."

"Clint."

"Clint," she said, pronouncing it correctly and not exaggerating it into Cleent.

"Why were you following me?"

"Because you caught my interest," she replied. "Not many of my brother's guests do."

"I'm flattered."

"You are the famous one," she said, placing her hand on his left arm, "the Gunsmith, no?"

"I suppose."

"I have never met a man such as you," she said, closing her hand over his left bicep. "Are you . . . different than other men?"

"In what way?" he asked.

She paused a moment and then said boldly, "In bed—in sssex!" she said, drawing out the 's' at the beginning of the word.

"How badly do you want to find out?" he asked, openly admiring her full-breasted figure.

She looked over her shoulder at the stand of trees he had been hidden behind, then wheeled her horse around and walked toward them. Clint pulled Duke's head around and followed her.

Behind the trees, she dismounted and immediately began to unbutton her shirt. He watched as she undressed. Her body was as dark as her face, with full, rounded breasts and very dark, distended nipples. The tangle of hair at her crotch was as black as the hair on her head.

"This badly," she said, placing her hands on her wide hips and spreading her legs so that he could just about see her excitement.

Clint unbuckled his gunbelt and laid it on the ground near them. Then he undressed while she watched, her nostrils flaring as her breathing quickened.

"*Dios!*" she said when his rigid, swollen penis came into view. "You are beautiful."

"No," he said, approaching her. "You are."

She took a few steps toward him, and he saw that she was almost as tall as he. The glistening head of his prick poked her in the stomach, and she reached down to caress it lovingly, stroking it gently with a feathery touch.

"*Muy bonito,*" she said, lowering herself to her knees so that she could roll his hard cock over her cheeks, flicking at it with her tongue as it passed her mouth. Suddenly, it was in her mouth, and her nails were biting into the flesh of his buttocks as she sucked on him. He looked down and saw her cheeks hollow out as she took all of him into her mouth.

He allowed her to do as she pleased with his cock until he felt as if he were going to explode. He wasn't quite ready for that yet. When that happened he wanted to be deep inside this hot-blooded woman.

"Carmen," he said, taking hold of her head and pulling himself free of her sucking mouth.

"No, por favor–" she said, reaching for him with her lips again.

"No," he said, putting his hands on her shoulder. Gently, he exerted pressure until she tumbled to the grassy knoll on her back.

"Spread your legs, Carmen," he said, "spread your beautiful legs."

"Si, my Gunsmith," she said breathlessly.

She spread her legs and he lowered his face to her wet, fragrant nest and probed with his tongue, savoring the taste of her before sliding his tongue up her slick lips to the stiff little nub that was the center of her pleasure.

"Oh, yes! Oh, please, lick it, suck it, bite it, my Gunsmith. Oooh, *hombre, si*—it is so good!"

He agreed. It was delicious! He flicked at her clit with his tongue until he felt her belly begin to tremble and then he sucked on it while her hips bounced and her body shook. Before her trembling stopped he took his long, hard cock and rammed it into her black bush.

She was long and sleek like Sally and as strong as Mary, yet neither of them could match the fullness of Carmen's figure. Her breasts and hips were like a cushion for him to lie upon while he stroked her hot furnace with his steel-hard poker.

"Oh *Dios! Si,* Clint, *si,* that is it. Oooh, harder, *por favor*—Ooh, *Madre de Dios!"*

He was coming inside of her, and she was pumping him, draining him, desperately seeking to drain him of every ounce of his seed and more, and then her own orgasm came and wracked her body with tremors of pure pleasure.

They had not kissed up to this point, so Clint eased his mouth onto hers, and she began to suck his tongue and chew his lips avidly, covering his face with moist kisses and moaning into his mouth as their orgasms subsided.

She grunted as he pulled out of her, stood up to get dressed.

"I have my answer, Clint Adams," she said, stretching languorously.

"Which is?"

"You are different from other men, my Gunsmith," she said, happily. "Very, very different."

Dressed, he reached down and took her hands, pulling her to her feet so that her full breasts were crushed against his chest.

"Mmm"," she moaned as he kissed her.

"We'll see each other again, Carmen."

"I am sure of that, my Gunsmith," she said as he mounted up to leave. "Very sure."

He rode away, leaving her there looking for all the world like she belonged there on that grassy knoll, naked among the trees.

"Hey, Gunsmith!" she called.

He turned his head and she said, "Town is that way," pointing in the opposite direction.

He smiled, turned his back, and kept riding.

NINETEEN

"You met her!"

Sally's statement was almost accusatory.

"Met who?"

"That bitch, Carmen."

"Sally—"

"I can smell her all over you."

"Why are you upset—"

"I'm not upset."

"Jeez, I'd hate to see you when you are then," he said, shifting Duke's reins from one hand to the other.

"Hank, take Clint's horse, please?" she called out to the jug-eared hand who was passing by.

"Yes, ma'am." He took the reins from Clint and said, "I'll treat him good."

"He'll take a piece out of you if you don't."

"What about you?" Sally asked as Hank led Duke to the barn.

"What about me?"

113

"Did Carmen take a piece out of you?"

"I thought we had an understanding—"

"Our understanding did not include that Mexican witch," Sally said. She turned and stormed into the house. He followed, a little amused.

"Why do I get the feeling you dislike Carmen Lujan?" he asked.

"I don't dislike her . . . I hate her!"

"Why?"

Sally glared at Clint for a few moments, and then he saw her make a physical effort to calm herself.

"All right," she said. "When I was . . . friendly with José, Carmen walked in on us once when we were . . . on the floor in his den."

"On the floor?" he asked, now more amused than before.

Looking sheepish Sally said, "You can get a lot . . . deeper that way. Anyway, she walked in and after that she started acting all high and mighty and said she didn't think I was good enough for her brother."

"Well, I can see where you'd dislike her for that."

"God," Sally said, sniffing the air, "you reek of her."

"I'll take a bath," he offered.

"Don't do that," she said in a resigned tone. "Tell me what happened with José."

"Not much. He says he had nothing to do with what happened last night, and I believe him."

"How can you be sure?"

"I'm not," he said, "but my hunch is he's telling the truth."

"What do we do now?"

"I don't know," Clint said, "I'm not a damn detective, Sally. How's your father?"

"He ate, but I practically had to feed him myself. I'm worried."

"We'll just have to figure out some way of making him want to get up and get well."

"We?"

"Well, I'm in this too—that is, if you still want me here."

"Of course I do," Sally said, "in fact, I think I want you here and now."

"On the floor?"

"If Pa wasn't in the house—" she said, but stopped short when she heard the sound of a horse approaching the house. "Now who's that?"

They walked to the front door and saw Sheriff Biegelheisen riding up.

"What could he want?" she wondered aloud.

"Let's wait and see if he tells us."

"He looks mad."

The little lawman slid down off his horse and approached the two of them. He was more than mad, he was furious.

"Miss, would you mind leaving me and Mr. Adams alone?"

"Yes, I would," she said, and the lawman seemed taken aback by her refusal.

"Miss Fountain, I'll remind you that I'm an officer of the law."

"I'll remind you, Sheriff, that you're on my father's land. This is my home. Anything you have to say to Mr. Adams can be said in front of me."

Helplessly, the man looked to Clint for assistance, but found none beyond a shrug.

"Very well, then," he said, and turned his attention to Clint. "I have just come from the Lujan ranch."

"Did you have some of his excellent brandy?"

"I don't drink when I'm doing my job, Mr. Adams."

"An admirable attitude, Sheriff."

"I'll be the judge of that," the sheriff said, using what was apparently his favorite phrase. "I didn't appreciate finding that you had been there before me questioning him about last night."

"I simply got an earlier start than you, Sheriff."

"Nevertheless, I must warn you to stay out of official business, Mr. Adams. I know your reputation, but you are no longer a lawman, and I must ask you to leave the enforcement of the law to me. Do I make myself clear?"

"Yes," Clint said.

"I do not like to threaten—"

"Then don't," Sally said, interrupting him. "You've had your say, Sheriff. Personally, I don't see what Clint did wrong. His life was in danger last night, and I think he has every right to try and find out who was doing the shooting."

"I'm working on that," the little lawman said stubbornly.

"Then I suggest you work on it somewhere else, Sheriff. You're not accomplishing anything here."

Biegelheisen was at a loss as to how to deal with Sally's retorts, so he simply glared at Clint and said, "Remember what I said, Adams."

"I promise."

The sheriff turned, mounted up, and rode away, his back stiff and straight.

"You were rough on him," Clint said.

"You should have stepped on him," she replied. "He's a nuisance."

"I'd sure like to know what kind of name that is, though," Clint said. "I'll have to ask him before I leave."

"We'll also have to try the floor before you leave," she reminded him.

"Definitely."

Later that day Ray Bogart was once again summoned to the office of his employer, who was pacing the floor as the gunman arrived.

"Problems?"

The man stopped pacing and turned to face Bogart.

"I've got another job for you."

"Adams?"

"Not yet. Something easier . . . and it may be only the beginning."

Dollar signs began to appear in front of Ray Bogart's eyes and he said, "Now you're talking my language."

Andre French left the bank by the rear door, which left him in the alley behind the building—a practice he always followed when he worked until after dark. He had done this so many times in the past that it did not even occur to him to look behind him as he started for the street.

When the knife sliced through the flesh of his back he gasped and tried to cry out, but the blood rising in his throat kept it down to an inaudible gurgle. The banker did the only thing he could do under the circumstances—he died.

TWENTY

The following morning Sally made breakfast for her father and forced him to eat, as she had done at dinner the night before. As she came out of his room with the empty tray she told Clint, "I'll have breakfast for you shortly."

"That's all right, Sally," he said, strapping on his gunbelt.

"Are you going out?"

"To town," he said, nodding. "I want to talk to Mills and French about what happened the other night. If Lujan wasn't behind it, one of them was."

"And Sam Wager?"

"Yeah, I'll be talking to Wager," Clint said, "but I'll save him for last."

"Be careful, Clint," Sally said, walking him to the door. "Whoever is behind it didn't think anything of killing two men."

"Don't worry, Sally," Clint said. "I haven't lived this long by not being careful."

"I'm sorry," she said, almost shyly. "I should know better than to say that to the Gunsmith."

He made a face and said, "I really wish you wouldn't call me that."

From inside they heard Andrew Fountain calling for her feebly and he said, "Go and take care of your father, and I'll see you in a while."

Clint walked to the stable, saddled Duke and gave the big black gelding his head back to town. Duke loved to run; he had more speed and stamina than any horse Clint had ever seen.

As Clint rode into town he noticed some sort of commotion over by the bank, and wondered if it had been robbed. He tied up Duke in front of the Whiskey River Saloon, and crossed the street to see what had happened.

The first person he saw was the sheriff, who was strutting about trying to look very official.

"Adams," the little man said when he spotted the Gunsmith. "What are you doing here?"

"Just rode into town, Sheriff," Clint replied. "What happened here?"

"Nothing that concerns you."

"Just curious, Sheriff. Maybe there's something I can do to help."

"This is a murder, Adams," Biegelheisen said, "and that makes it my business, not yours."

"Murder? Who was murdered?"

Before the sheriff could reply, a harried looking young lady stepped forward and blurted out, "It was my boss, Mr. French. He was stabbed!"

"Miss Ivy—" the sheriff started to say, but he was cut off by Clint.

"Andre French was killed?" he said, seeking verification.

"That's right," the woman said. "It was horrible."

Clint recognized the woman now as French's assistant.

"You found the body, ma'am?"

"I did," she said. "It was horrible." She started to cry.

"Adams," the lawman snapped, imposing his small body between the Gunsmith and the weeping woman. "I'll ask the questions, if you don't mind!"

"I don't mind at all, Sheriff," Clint said. "Go ahead and ask."

The little lawman turned to face the woman, who was still crying. He seemed at a loss as to how to conduct himself with a woman.

"Where did you find him?" Clint asked over the sheriff's shoulder.

"In the alley behind the bank."

"What would he be doing back there?"

"He often l-left that way when h-he worked late at n-night," she said, sniffling. "He was afraid that if he l-left by the front door the bank might get robbed."

Biegelheisen whirled angrily on Clint, who

held his hands up in front of him and backed away.

"Sorry, Sheriff," he said, "but I'm only trying to be of some assistance."

Biegelheisen turned to French's assistant and said, "Miss Ivy, would you accompany me to my office, please, where we could be more comfortable while we talk?"

"Of c-course."

"Don't forget to ask if anyone heard the shot," Clint reminded the sheriff.

"That shows how much you know, Adams," the man sneered at him, "because French wasn't shot, he was stabbed!"

"My mistake," Clint said, and the sheriff, accompanied by the blubbering Miss Ivy, started for his office, unaware of the satisfied look on Clint Adams' face.

Clint walked across the street to retrieve Duke from in front of the Whiskey River Saloon when the saloon doors opened and Sam Wager stepped out. He spotted Clint and stepped out onto the boardwalk.

"What's all the commotion?" he asked, his tone glaringly conversational.

"It seems that a friend of yours was murdered late last night."

"A friend of mine?" Wager repeated, frowning, "Who?"

"You don't know?"

"No, I don't."

"And I suppose you also don't know anything about two men being killed out at the Fountain ranch two night ago?"

"No," Wager said, very carefully, "I don't. Do I have to go across to the bank myself and—" Wager started to say, but he stopped short as realization apparently came to him. "Andre!"

"Good guess," Clint said, "although what an Irishman was doing with a name like that I'll never know."

"Ben Williams, and Jud Clark, and now Andre French—all dead."

"Kind of narrows the field down a bit," Clint said, "doesn't it? Or maybe that's just what somebody has in mind, eh Wager? Somebody with a lot of . . . ambition?"

"I don't know what you're talking about," Wager said. He backed up toward the saloon entrance, groping for it without looking.

"Your Salt Ring is gradually growing smaller and smaller, Wager," Clint said, "and it's not by accident."

"And you think it's my doing?"

"As I said, the field is narrowing," Clint said. "The only ones left are Fountain, Mills, Lujan, and you, only as far as I'm concerned, Lujan is in the clear."

"Why do you say that?"

"Because somebody went through a whole lot of trouble to make me believe otherwise, and I'm not buying."

123

"You're forgetting something, Adams. Those three are all part of the El Paso Republicans. So were the dead men. I'm not."

"Not yet," Clint said, taking hold of Duke's reins, "but I happen to know that there are a few openings."

Clint left Duke at the livery and walked to the law office of William Mills. He had more to use on the Salt Ring members now to try and get the guilty one to crack. First, there was the fact that he didn't believe that Lujan was behind the shooting at the Fountain house. Second, there was the murder of Andre French.

With Fountain in bed and Lujan temporarily in the clear, Clint had only two suspects now, Wager and Mills. He'd already let Wager know that the setup hadn't worked, and now he was going to tell Mills the same thing.

Ray Bogart stepped out of the café and saw Clint Adams walking down El Paso Street. How easy it would have been to just step out into the street and get it over with, but that wasn't what he was being paid to do, so he stepped back into the doorway to avoid being seen.

Clint entered Mills's office, shut the door behind him, and studied the man behind the desk for traces of drunkenness.

"Mr. Adams," Mills said, standing up, "I'm glad you stopped by."

"Why is that, Mr. Mills?"

"I want to apologize for my behavior the other day," Mills said. "It was intolerable. I was, uh, a little drunk, you see—"

"I noticed," Clint said, "but that's never been a major crime, Mr. Mills, so don't worry about it."

"Thank you. Won't you have a seat?"

"I can talk standing up."

"Very well."

"Have you looked out your window this morning?"

"I noticed something going on in front of the bank," Mills admitted. "Do you know anything about it?"

"Yes, I do, as a matter of fact. I just finished speaking to Sam Wager about it."

"Sam? What has he to do with it?"

"Both he and you are minus a friend this morning," Clint said. "That is, if either one of you considered Andre French a friend."

"Andre was my partner, Mr. Adams. But why are we talking about him as if he were—" Mills said, and then stopped short.

"Dead?" Clint finished for him. "Because he is, Mr. Mills. Somebody stuck a knife in him last night."

"That's terrible," Mills said, sitting back in his chair as if stunned by the news. "I . . . I assume, then, that the bank was robbed."

"Why would you assume that?"

"Well, I just . . . I just figured that with Andre

being bank manager—"

Although he didn't have any way of knowing whether or not the bank had been robbed, Clint said, "French's death had nothing to do with the bank, Mr. Mills. His murder was for personal reasons."

"But who would want to kill Andre?"

"That's a good question. The sheriff is looking into that, I believe."

Mills snorted and said, "That dentist! Why we ever agreed to appoint him sheriff I'll never be able to understand." Mills looked at Clint with a frown and asked, "What is your connection with the investigation of Andre's death, Mr. Adams?"

"I have no connection," Clint replied. "In fact, I've been warned away by the sheriff."

"I see. Are you still staying out at the Fountain house?"

"Oh, yes."

"How is Andy getting along."

"Quite well," Clint lied. "He'll be back on his feet in no time at all."

"That's good to hear. I should go out and see if he and Sally need any help."

"Oh, I'll pass the message along," Clint said. "I don't really think that going out there would be all that good of an idea."

"Why not? Andy is my friend."

"I'm not really that sure of that, Mr. Mills," Clint said, "and since it's my intent to keep Mr. Fountain healthy, I'd advise you to stay in town if I were you."

Mills stood up slowly and said, "Are you threatening me, Adams?"

"I'm giving you some damn good advice, Mills," Clint replied, moving toward the door. "If I were you, I'd take it."

TWENTY-ONE

Leaving Mills's office, Clint noticed José Lujan's sister standing across the street in front of the General Store next to a buckboard, and crossed over.

"Carmen."

She whirled around gracefully at the sound of her name and then smiled when she saw who it was.

"Clint? How nice. What are you doing in town?"

"Just some business. You?"

"The same. I have to pick up some supplies."

"Don't you have hands to do that?"

She laughed and said, "I am living in my brother's house, and every so often I feel the need to earn my keep."

"Admirable, and speaking of your brother—"

"Yes?"

"I wonder if you would give him a message for me."

"Of course."

"Tell him that Andre French was murdered last night, stabbed in the back."

"*Dios,* how terrible!" she said, her shock genuine.

"Yes. He'll be very interested to know about it."

"I am sure he will," she agreed. "I will tell him."

As he started to turn she put her hand on his arm and said, "Must you leave town immediately?"

"I'm afraid so."

"I was hoping we could . . . be curious together again, perhaps this time on something softer than the ground."

"Oh, I don't know," he said, watching her face. "A friend once told me that it's better on something hard—like a floor."

Something flickered across her face. "I see."

"Perhaps another time."

"I hope so."

"I'm sure of it."

"Andre's dead?" Andrew Fountain repeated, staring at Clint in disbelief.

"I'm afraid so, sir."

"Then there are only four of us left."

"Yes," Clint said, looking across the bed at Sally, who sat on the other side, her hand on her father's arm.

"Mr. Fountain," Clint said, "has it ever occurred to you that this may be the work of someone outside your Salt Ring?"

"Such as who?"

"Someone who would benefit from seeing the Ring fall apart," Clint suggested.

"I suppose—"

"Do you know of someone?"

"I know a lot of people," Fountain said. "There were plenty of men who were making a living taking salt out of the beds near Guadalupe Peak before we organized our business."

"Could you give me a couple of their names or the name of someone I could talk to who might represent those people?"

"Sure," he said. Talk to Hector Rio."

"Hector Rio," Clint repeated.

"Ride out towards the Peak, and when you come within sight of it, head west. You'll come to a small shack which is where you'll find Rio."

"I'll take him," Sally offered.

"You will not!" Fountain snapped, with the first sign of life in quite some time.

"Why not?" Sally demanded.

Fountain looked at Clint and said, "If Rio doesn't know you, he's liable to shoot first when you ride up on him, so be careful." He turned to his daughter and said, "I don't want you anywhere near Rio. He hates me and wouldn't be above harming you to get to me."

"Or killing your partners?" Clint asked.

The old man turned his glance back to Clint. "I guess not, but you'll remember that Ben Williams killed Jud Clark, and I killed Ben Williams."

"Someone instigated Williams's actions that night," Clint reasoned. "Would it have to be one of the partners?"

"I suppose not," Fountain said. "It was no secret that Ben didn't feel he was getting his fair share of the profits from the Salt Ring."

"All right, then," Clint said. "I'll talk to Hector Rio. Sally, could you come outside and point me in the right direction?"

"Sure. I'll be back in a moment with your lunch, Pa."

"Good," Fountain said to her surprise, "I'm hungry enough to eat it."

Outside she said, "I'm sorry Andre's dead, but his death seems to have kicked some life into Pa."

"I noticed. Maybe he figures the killer is getting closer to him now."

"Who do you think it is?"

"I don't know, Sally. Maybe I'll know something after I've spoken to this Hector Rio. Which way is the Peak?"

She pointed and gave him directions and he pulled Duke over and mounted up.

"Get him his lunch while he's feeling feisty, and I'll see you both later."

TWENTY-TWO

Following Fountain's directions, he turned Duke's head west when the Peak came into view, and after about fifteen minutes came within sight of a shack.

"Okay, Duke," he said to the big horse while dismounting, "I'm going to leave you here because he's sure to hear those big feet of yours."

Duke gave Clint a baleful look, and Clint said, "Don't get insulted. Go off and wait for me now."

He walked the rest of the distance to the shack. The structure wasn't much more than a line shack, big enough for a cot, a table, a man, and not much more. He moved to one of the windows and peered in. There was a man on a cot, and he appeared to be asleep.

"So much the better," he muttered to himself, and moved towards the front door. Gingerly he tested the door, found it unlocked, and opened it silently.

The sleeping man had a gun within reach, and Clint moved quickly and quietly to remove it. Then he woke the man by prodding him with his finger.

"Eh," the man muttered, *"qué pasa–"*

"Rise and shine, amigo."

The man's eyes fluttered open, danced about the room and eventually came to a stop on the face of the Gunsmith. His hand moved quickly towards his gun, and Clint let him find out for himself that it wasn't there.

"Who are you?" the man asked.

"Someone who wants to talk."

"About what?"

"The salt beds."

The man said something rude in Spanish, and even though Clint didn't understand the language, he knew a rude remark when he heard it.

"Why don't you sit up real slow like," he suggested to the man, "so we can get acquainted."

The man sat up, and Clint got a better look at him. The Mexican was in his thirties, built lean and hard with a long, unshaven jaw and blood-shot black eyes.

"Are you Hector Rio?"

"Si."

"My name is Clint Adams."

"Do you work for the Salt Ring?" Rio asked, bypassing Clint's name without a flicker of recognition.

"No," Clint said.

"What do you want from me, Señor? I have no money at all, and very little food—"

"I told you, I want to talk."

Clint could see a gleam in the man's eye. "Talking is very thirsty work," he said, licking his lips.

"Do you have anything around here?"

"No," the man said sadly.

"Well, I didn't bring a bottle, but I'm sure I could scrape up the price of one."

"It is also something that brings on hunger," the man pointed out.

"That could be arranged too, amigo. Are we going to talk?"

"What about?"

Clint sighed and said, "I told you, the salt beds."

"Talk."

"Are you the leader of the people who are opposing the Salt Ring?"

"I am not their leader," Hector replied, "but they listen to me."

"Would they listen to you if you told them to kill someone?"

"Kill!" Hector blurted. "I do not understand. I heard that Williams and Clark had been killed, but they killed each other, did they not?"

"That's true enough," Clint said, "but the same can't be said for Andre French."

"Someone killed the banker?" Hector said, looking surprised.

"Last night."

"How?"

"He was stabbed. Do you own a knife, Hector?"

"I use a gun, Señor."

"Uh-huh," Clint said, knowing that the remark meant nothing.

"Is this what you want to talk to me about, Señor?" Hector asked then, displaying more intelligence than Clint would have given him credit for. "You want to know if I killed the banker?"

"Did you?"

"I would have done so gladly," Hector Rio said, standing up and sticking out his chest proudly, "but I did not."

"What about the others?"

"The others who have been cheated by the banker and the Salt Ring?" Hector asked. He shrugged and said, "You would have to ask them."

"Couldn't you ask them and let me know?"

"For the price of some food and a drink."

Clint took the price of some food and a bottle out of his pocket and handed it to the man.

"That's the beginning, Hector," he said. "Bring me some answers, and there will be more."

"You want to know who killed the banker?"

"I want to know if any of your people did it," Clint said, "If so, I don't have to know who he is. That's for the sheriff to find out. Not knowing the answer will make what I have to do a lot easier."

He knew that Hector Rio would not betray one of his people for money, but if all he had to do was find out if one of them killed French without having to name the man, that was another story.

"Si, Señor," Hector said finally, tucking the money away in his pocket. "I will do as you ask. I do not think any of us have killed the banker, but I will ask."

"I'm staying at the Fountain ranch, Hector. You can find me there when you have the answer, or leave it with Sally Fountain."

"I will be shot on sight if I appear there."

"No, you won't," Clint assured him. "I'll see to that. Do we have an agreement?"

Hector thought a moment, then nodded and said, "We have an agreement, Señor."

"Good," Clint said.

He took the man's gunbelt off the chair he'd hung it on and tossed it to him. Without hesitating Hector Rio strapped it on, then proceeded to ignore it.

"Por favor, Señor," Hector said as he saw Clint watching him carefully, "I am not so foolish as to think that I can best the gringo legend with a gun."

Rio knew who he was. Well, maybe that would make the agreement more solid. There was no fear in the man's face, but there was respect.

And that was the only part of being a legend that Clint didn't mind so much.

● ● ●

Ray Bogart was about to go upstairs with his favorite little saloon girl when a kid ran in with a message that he was wanted. Bogart didn't need to be told by whom.

"Sorry, darlin'," he said, patting the girl on her firm behind. "Maybe later."

"Sure," she replied, almost too quickly.

Bogart walked over to his employer's office, wondering if it was finally time for him to be turned loose on the Gunsmith.

The man looked worried when Bogart arrived, and hastily tucked a whiskey bottle away in a drawer of his desk when the gunman entered the room.

Who did he think he was kidding? Certainly not Ray Bogart.

"Can't get courage out of a bottle, you know," Bogart commented. "It just ain't there."

"I don't need the courage," the other man replied peevishly. "You do."

"What's the problem?"

"Clint Adams is getting too close," the man said.

It's your own fault, Bogart thought, for narrowing the field down. Bogart had heard some talk in town about the Salt Ring, and thought he had his employer pretty well figured out. An ambitious man who had too many partners. Well naturally, when partners started dying, the other partners came under suspicion. It couldn't be avoided, and if the Gunsmith was the only man who was a danger, then he had to be done away with before the last partner was.

"You figure it's time?" Bogart asked.

The man ran his hand over the lower portion of his face in a nervous gesture and said, "Are you sure you can take him?"

"I'm sure."

"If you don't, he'll come after me."

"You should have thought of that before you got involved."

"It would have gone fine if Adams hadn't come to town," the man complained. "It would have gone off without a hitch."

"Nothing goes off without a hitch," Bogart said. "When do you want it done?"

"The first chance you get."

"It's going to be done fair," Bogart said. "No knives in the back."

"Do it whatever way you want to," the other man said, "but get it done."

"Fair—" Bogart said, "that's the only way a legend should die."

TWENTY-THREE

It was Sam Wager who called for the meeting the next day.

There were two schools of thought on this. Sally said he was doing it to throw suspicion off himself. Clint said he could be doing it simply because he was innocent and scared.

"It has to be Sam," Sally maintained. "The only person in the world he's afraid of is his wife."

"Why is that?"

"She's one of the leaders of the Women's Social League, active in the church," Sally explained. "If she left him, it would kill him politically."

They were in Andrew Fountain's room, discussing the fact that Sam Wager had just called a meeting of the Salt Ring.

"Pa?" Sally said, looking for her father's view.

"I don't know if it's Sam or not," the old man said, "but I do know I'm going to that meeting.

Where did that messenger say it was going to be held?"

"That's odd, too," Clint said. "It's going to be held at the Slash-J tonight at eight."

"I'm going to ride into town and tell Sam to hold it here," Sally said.

"Nonsense," Fountain said, pushing back the bed covers, "I can get to Lujan's ranch."

Sally looked at Clint with barely concealed glee in her eyes, then rushed to her father's bedside and said the precise thing that would make him even more anxious to get up.

"You can't go. You're still hurt."

"Get away from me, girl!" he snarled. He put his feet on the floor and stood up. For a moment he swayed, but Clint motioned Sally back, and the old man eventually steadied himself.

"See?" he said triumphantly.

"Fine," Sally said. "Now get back in bed until later this evening. Clint and I will go with you to the meeting."

"No, you won't," he said, sitting back down on the bed. "No one is allowed at a Salt Ring or Republican meeting unless he's a member."

"You can't go if we don't go with you," Sally insisted. The old man looked to Clint for assistance.

"I agree with her, Mr. Fountain," Clint said, "except for one thing."

"What?" she demanded hotly.

"I'll go with him, and you stay in town."

"This is ridiculous—" Fountain began, but Clint cut him short.

"Mr. Fountain, if Wager is the man behind the deaths, this may be a way to lure you away from here, and away from my protection. I can't allow that—that is, unless you're ready to do without my protection."

The old man seemed to mull that over for a few moments, then grunted and agreed, adding, "But you do like he says, girl, and wait in town. If there's any shooting, I don't want you around."

She glared at both men in turn, then stormed out of the room.

"What do you think?" Clint asked him.

"I don't think you'll get her to stay in town unless you have the sheriff lock her in jail."

"Considering my relationship with the sheriff, I don't see that as an alternative," Clint said. "I'll just have to talk to her."

"You go ahead, then," Fountain said. "Lord knows I haven't had much luck with her since her mother died. I swear, some of the things that girl does . . ." Fountain said, trailing off and shaking his head.

"I'm sure she has her reasons for the things she does, like we all do, sir," Clint offered. "Maybe one of these days you should ask her."

"Maybe I should, Adams," Andrew Fountain said. "By golly, maybe I should."

"He dozed off," Clint said as he found Sally

Fountain on the front porch, "but I think he's going to be all right."

"I hope so," she said. "Now let's discuss this nonsense about me staying in town."

Clint studied her, arms folded in front of her and feet solidly planted, and wondered just how much luck he would have arguing with her. What he would probably have to do was outsmart her.

"What about Carmen?" he asked.

"What!" she said, thrown off balance by the question.

"If you go to Lujan's, you'll have to see his sister."

She made a face and was about to protest, when a rider approached.

As the rider came closer it became obvious that it was a woman.

"Who's she?" Sally wondered aloud.

Clint saw that the woman was barely big enough to control the animal she was riding, and it wasn't hard to guess who she was.

"It's Mary Randall," Clint said.

"Who?" Sally asked, and then said, "Oh, you must mean your other girl friend?"

"Yes."

Mary Randall pulled her horse to a stop in front of the porch. Clint stepped forward to help her and lifted her from the saddle, setting her down on the ground easily.

"Mary, do you know Sally Fountain?"

"We've seen each other in town," Sally said,

stepping off the porch, "but I guess we never had enough in common to meet—until now."

Mary saw that the look on Sally's face was at least amiable and said, "Hello, Miss Fountain."

"Oh, just call me Sally, Mary," she said, and to Clint's relief the women shook hands.

"What brings you out here?" Clint asked.

"Something I thought you should know. There's been a man coming to the saloon the past few days and I've been spending some time with him," Mary said, casting a sidelong glance at Sally.

"Go on, Mary," Clint said.

"Well, I didn't know who he was until today, when I heard another man in the saloon say so."

"And?" Clint said, prompting her.

"He's a gunman named Ray Bogart."

"Bogart!"

"Do you know him?" Sally asked.

"I know of him," Clint said, rubbing his jaw thoughtfully. "He's a hired killer."

"Why would he be here?" Mary asked. Clint and Sally exchanged glances. "For you?"

"Possibly," Clint said.

"What can I do to help?" Mary asked, immediately recognizing that there was more going on then she knew about.

"You can point Bogart out to Sally, here, and then you can both keep an eye on him this evening," Clint replied.

"In town?" Sally said, knowing that Clint had

finally found a way to keep her in El Paso and away from the meeting at the Lujan place.

"As long as he stays there," Clint says. "If he leaves, Sally, you'll have to follow him."

"That would be no problem."

"You'd have to be very careful he doesn't see you, though," Clint added.

"I know that."

"What else can I do?" Mary asked.

Clint looked down at her and asked, "Have you seen him and your boss together?"

"Bogart and Sam?" she repeated, thinking it over. "Not that I can remember."

"Then just go back to town now, and Sally will be in later."

"All right, Clint."

She turned and Clint lifted her into the saddle, letting his hand rest on one of her marvelous thighs.

"Thanks for coming out here to tell me."

"I was worried," she said frankly. "I couldn't think of anyone else who should know more than you."

"I'll see you later in town," he assured her.

"Be careful."

"I'll see you later, Mary," Sally called out.

"I'll be waiting," Mary said.

As she wheeled her horse around and started back to town Clint said, "You like her?"

"You like her," Sally said, "so she must be worth liking."

"That's the nicest thing anyone's ever said to me."

"Don't let it go to your head," Sally advised him. "When she and I get through comparing notes, you may be in a lot of trouble."

TWENTY-FOUR

Clint and Andrew Fountain arrived for the meeting at the Slash-J early.

They had left the Fountain ranch at the same time as Sally. Fountain rode in a buckboard, since he was still unable to sit a horse, and Clint followed him on Duke.

"Don't forget," Clint told Sally, wishing that he had someone else to send in her place, "if you have to follow Bogart, don't let him see you."

"Don't worry," Sally said, "you two just take care of yourselves."

"And don't try anything clever," Clint added.

"Like what?"

Fountain interrupted them by laughing and said, "I think Clint knows you like a book, girl."

"Just do what I've told you to do and nothing more," Clint told her.

"Yes, sir," she said, giving him a mock salute.

When Sally arrived in town she hurriedly left

her horse at the livery, leaving instructions with the boy there to keep the animal ready to leave at a moment's notice. After that she walked to the Whiskey River Saloon.

Upon entering she spotted Mary Randall seated at a table with a man. Wondering if he was Ray Bogart, she walked to the bar and ordered a beer.

A few seconds later Mary appeared beside her and asked the bartender for two drinks.

"Is that him?" Sally asked.

"No," Mary said. "When Bogart comes in I'll touch my left ear and approach him right away."

As Mary turned with the drinks in her hands Sally said, "What if he doesn't show up? What if he goes to the meeting instead?"

Mary was considering the question when the batwing doors swung open, and a man walked in.

"We won't have to worry about that," she told Sally.

"Why not?"

"Because," Mary said in a low but urgent tone, "he just walked in!"

"Ah, Andrew my friend," José Lujan said, hurrying down the steps to meet his partner. "It is wonderful to see you on your feet again. The last time we saw each other you did not look at all well."

"I'm fine, José," Fountain told him, stepping down from the buckboard with assistance from Clint. "Just fine."

"And Clint," Lujan continued, "you are always welcome in my home, amigo, but I must inform you that no one is permitted to attend these meetings but members."

"That's bull," Fountain said firmly. "Clint is with me, José, and if he doesn't come in, I don't."

"As you wish, Andrew," Lujan said, spreading his arms in a helpless gesture, "but I fear the others will raise an objection or two."

"That's too bad," Fountain said and strode past Lujan up the steps and into the house.

Sally knew that Clint's reputation was greater than Ray Bogart's, but Clint did not look the part and Bogart did. He was tall, mean-looking, almost ugly—and yet she knew that his crudeness, combined with the air of danger he carried with him, would make him appeal to women.

At one time, he might even have appealed to Sally Fountain—but not anymore.

She watched as Bogart took a table and beckoned to Mary. The man she had been sitting with apparently knew who Bogart was, for he raised no objection when she left him to go to the gunman's table.

Sally took her beer to a corner table, where she settled down to wait.

"I'm glad you came tonight," Mary said to Ray Bogart.

"Why?"

"Because I missed you."

"Sure," Bogart laughed, "and I missed you,

too, honey. Maybe we should get married, huh?"

"No," Mary said, "not married, but we could start by going upstairs."

"Listen," he said, grabbing her arm in a painful grip, "don't forget who's paying here, little lady. I say when we go upstairs."

"Sure. I was just—"

"Right. Now I want a drink," he added, releasing her arm, "and that's for starters!"

Ray Bogart watched Mary walk to the bar for his drinks, wondering why she was suddenly being so friendly when all along she'd been so businesslike.

Lujan hurried into the house after Fountain, with Clint trailing along.

"The others haven't arrived yet," Lujan said to Fountain, "but we can start with a glass of brandy."

"Fine," Fountain said, waiting for his host to lead the way.

When they each had a glass, Clint decided to retreat to a corner of the room, where he could watch. He would not take part in any discussion unless he was called upon to do so.

"I wonder what Sam has in mind—" Lujan began, but he was stopped by a knock on the door. "I will have to get that myself," he said, setting down his glass. "I instructed Carmen to stay in her room."

"Obedient girl," Fountain said, obviously

thinking about Sally, who definitely did not match that description.

Lujan returned in moments with Sam Wager, who stopped short as he entered the room and saw Clint Adams.

"What the hell is *he* doing here?" he demanded, turning on his host. Lujan simply spread his hands and shrugged.

"You will have to ask Andrew."

"Andy," Wager said, looking at the old man seated on the sofa, "you know these meetings are only open to members."

"Bull," Fountain said, again. "You know that we discuss Republican business here, but do we ask you to leave because you're not a member?"

"That's different—"

"If Adams goes, I go," Fountain said firmly. "You called this meeting, so you decide."

"Ah—" Wager said, and there was another knock on the door.

"That will be William," Lujan said, and hurried to let Mills in.

When Williams Mills entered, he cast a glance at Clint Adams, but said nothing and hurried to the brandy decanter to pour himself a drink.

Thus armed he turned and said, "All right, Sam, you called this meeting. What's it about?"

"It's about Ben Williams, Jud Clark, and Andre French," the saloon owner replied.

"They are all dead," José Lujan said, standing by the fireplace with his elbow on the mantle.

"Exactly," Sam Wager said, "and who knows which of us will be next?"

"Why should any of us be next?" Mills demanded. "Ben and Jud died as a result of an unfortunate . . . incident, which almost cost Andy his life as well—but that's all it was."

"And Andre?" Wager asked.

"Maybe someone wanted to rob the bank but was frightened away after killing Andre."

"Frightened by what?" Wager demanded. "They were alone in a dark alley. No, Will. Somebody killed him—or had him killed—and we could be next."

"Nonsense!" Mills said, pouring himself another drink. It was obvious that he must have had a few even before he arrived.

"What do you think, Andrew?" Lujan asked.

"I agree with Sam," the older man said. "Somebody is trying to kill us."

"And they're succeeding."

"Clint," Lujan said, seeking to draw the Gunsmith into the conversation, "do you have an opinion?"

Wager seemed about to protest, but then apparently decided that he was interested in what the Gunsmith had to say on the subject and held his peace.

"Does anyone object to my voicing an opinion?" Clint asked the room at large. When no one did, he continued. "All right, then. I agree with

Sam Wager. I think someone is out to kill off the members of the El Paso Salt Ring and/or Republicans."

"Hah!" Wager said triumphantly.

"Further," Clint continued, "I think that the guilty party is right here in this room."

"One of us?" Mills demanded.

Clint nodded.

"I think one of you fine gentlemen is out to go into business for himself."

Sally Fountain took another small sip of her lukewarm beer and felt her eyes beginning to grow heavy. Still, she had to remain alert for any movement on the part of Ray Bogart. When he pushed his chair back to get up, her heart began to pound. If he headed for the door, she'd have to get up and follow him.

Bogart stood up, wavered a moment, stretched, and then took hold of Mary's arm and started towards the stairs leading to the second floor.

Sally breathed a sigh of relief, then felt an immediate surge of guilt. She was safe down here while Mary had to go upstairs with Bogart, but then that was her job, wasn't it? If she wasn't going up there with him, she'd probably be going with another man.

Sally got up, went to the bar and got another beer. She took it back to her table, sat down and kept her eyes on the stairway. If Bogart suddenly appeared, she wanted to be ready.

An attitude of suspicion permeated the room as the Gunsmith's last statement hung in the air. Silently, the four remaining partners regarded each other, and it was William Mills who broke the silence.

"How do we know it isn't you?" he asked Clint.

"Are you saying I hired Clint to kill my partners?" Andrew Fountain asked.

"Of course not, Andy, but Adams has a reputation as a gunman—"

"He's here to keep me alive until we find out who's behind this nonsense," Fountain said, "and he's not being paid for it. His gun is not for hire!"

"I'm tired of this," Mills said, putting his empty glass down. "I'm sorry, Sam, but we're not accomplishing anything here but becoming suspicious of each other."

"If that's the case," Fountain said, "then we've accomplished quite a lot."

Mills shook his head and walked out of the room. Wager looked as if he wanted to say something, but then he too shook his head, put down his empty glass, and left.

"I guess the meeting's over," Fountain said, struggling to his feet without assistance. "Let's go, Clint."

He started for the door and Clint followed.

"Clint," Lujan called.

"Yes?"

The Mexican crossed the room to stand next to him and asked, "How much it would it cost for you to work for me and look into this?"

"You've got the wrong man, José," Clint said. "I'm just here helping a friend."

"Then perhaps I should hire someone else."

"Maybe you should," Clint said. That is, if you haven't already paid Ray Bogart, he added to himself.

Halfway back to the Fountain ranch Clint called for Andrew Fountain to stop.

"What is it?"

"I want to go to town and get Sally out of the Whiskey River Saloon. When Sam Wager gets there he might—"

"I understand, young feller," Fountain said, interrupting him. "You go on ahead."

"You'll be all right?"

"I'll be fine."

"I don't think anyone will try anything tonight."

"Let 'em," Fountain said fiercely. "I'm ready to fight for my life, boy."

"Sally will be glad to hear that."

"Well, you go on and get her, and I'll tell her myself."

"Yes, sir," Clint said. "See you back at the ranch."

TWENTY-FIVE

Sally didn't see Sam Wager walk into the saloon. She still had her eyes glued to the stairway, waiting for some sign of Ray Bogart.

Wager saw her though, and immediately walked over to her table.

"Sally."

She jerked her head around in surprise, eyes wide. When she saw that it was Wager, she relaxed.

"Sam."

"Waiting for me?"

"No, Sam. I'm just relaxing."

Wager looked around the room, which had emptied considerably, and said, "It's getting late, Sally. Why don't you come into my office and relax with me."

"No, thank you, Sam."

"Maybe I should stop asking," he said, grabbing hold of her arm, "and start telling." He

159

pulled her to her feet, and as he did they both heard a scream from upstairs.

"What the hell—" Wager said.

"Mary's up there," Sally said.

There was another scream, which was cut off abruptly, and Wager dropped Sally's arm and started for the stairs.

"She's the best girl I've got," he was muttering. "If some broken down cowboy has hurt her—"

"Sam," Sally called out. She wanted to warn him that it was Ray Bogart up there, but Wager was too intent on getting upstairs before Mary could become severely damaged goods.

"Open up in there!" Wager demanded, pounding on Mary's door.

"Help! Sam!" Mary called from inside. Sally had moved to the foot of the steps where she could see and hear everything.

"Goddamn it!" Wager swore. He raised his fist to pound on the door again when suddenly there was a shot and something punched him in the chest right through the door. He staggered backwards a few feet, his knees gave way, and he fell to the floor.

Sally ran over to the bar and scrambled behind it. Whatever customers had been left in the place had run out when they heard the shot, including the bartender.

Crouched behind the bar she peered at the stairs and saw Ray Bogart come out of Mary's room, still holding his gun. He stared down at

Sam Wager, then stepped over him and came down the stairs. Sally ducked all the way down behind the bar, and when she looked up again, Bogart was gone.

She hurried out from behind the bar and ran up the stairs. She paused as she encountered Sam Wager's body, then stepped over it and hurried into Mary's room.

The tiny saloon girl was crumpled on the floor next to the bed, sobbing.

"Mary!" Sally cried, rushing to her side. When Mary looked up at her, Sally saw that her lip was cut and that there was a bruise deepening on her right cheekbone.

"Are you all right?"

"Yes," Mary said. "I thought he was going to kill me."

"What happened?" Sally asked. "Why did he start to beat you up?"

"He said I was too friendly all of a sudden, and he wanted to know why. When I told him I didn't know what he was talking about, he started to hit me."

"What happened here?" a voice asked from behind them.

Both girls looked up and were relieved to see that the speaker was Clint Adams.

"Clint!" Mary called.

He rushed over and squatted down next to both women.

"Are you two all right?"

"I'm fine," Sally said, "but Bogart beat Mary up."

Clint examined Mary's face by putting two fingers under her chin and tilting it up. He kissed her gently on the head.

"What happened to Wager?" he asked.

"When he heard Mary calling for help he rushed upstairs and started banging on the door. Bogart shot him right through the door!"

"Bogart shot him?"

"Yes," Mary said.

"Come on, Mary," Clint said, taking her by the upper arms. "Sit on the bed. Sally, get a damp rag so we can clean her face."

"I thought he was going to kill me," Mary said again, this time to Clint.

"Don't worry," Clint said. "He's not going to kill you. He's not going to hurt you anymore."

"Clint," she whispered, and leaned her head against his chest. When Sally came back with the damp cloth, Clint used it to clean Mary's lip.

"I guess the sheriff will be here soon," Sally said.

"Oh, hell," Clint said, "not him. He'll try to bring Bogart in and get himself killed doing it."

"And what about you?" Sally asked.

"What do you mean?"

"Are you going after Bogart?"

"Bogart and the man who hired him."

"Well," Sally said, "at least we know it wasn't Sam—unless he didn't know it was Sam outside the door and accidentally killed him."

"No," Mary said, "when I heard Sam's voice I called out to him. Bogart said to me, 'That's your boss coming to save his merchandise,' and then he fired through the door. He knew who it was."

"And he wouldn't kill the man who was paying him," Clint said. "Not unless he was crazy. I've heard a lot things about Bogart, but I've never heard that he was crazy."

"So then which one is it?" Sally asked. "William Mills or José Lujan?"

"Time enough for that tomorrow," Clint said, taking hold of Mary again. "Let's get Mary out of here before the sheriff comes."

"We'll take her to the ranch, where she won't have to worry about Ray Bogart," Sally said, and Clint was glad that she had been the one to suggest it.

"Good idea."

They grabbed some clothes for her and the three of them hurried down the back way and out the door. They made their way to the livery without being seen, got Sally's horse, and Clint took Mary on Duke with him. The big black barely noticed the extra weight.

"Are you going after Bogart tomorrow, Clint?" Sally asked Clint as they rode out of town.

"I think this whole thing will be over tomorrow, Sally," Clint said.

"Will you turn him over to the sheriff?"

Clint looked over at Sally and said, "That'll be up to him."

Andrew Fountain welcomed Mary Randall

into his home, and Sally gave up her bed so that the frightened, battered, and bruised young woman could get a good night's sleep.

Clint went outside to talk to the men in the bunkhouse, and they agreed to take turns standing watch by twos after Clint told them it was what Fountain—and Sally—wanted. It was obvious to him that all four men were in love with Sally Fountain to some degree, and loyal to Andrew.

As he was returning to the house, he heard someone call his name and looked around. Finally, he spotted Hector Rio standing in the bushes, beckoning to him.

"I have been waiting for you to return," Rio said.

"Why didn't you go inside? I told you no one would shoot you."

"I wished to play it, how you say, the safe way," Hector said. Clint couldn't blame him for that.

"Do you have something to tell me?"

"I have nothing to tell you," Hector said.

"Which means?"

"My people had nothing to do with the banker's death, but they are all glad in their hearts that he is dead. They say that they hope the others will die soon, too."

"Well, I'm doing my best to see that doesn't happen," Clint said.

Hector Rio shrugged and said, "We each do what we must do."

"Will you or your people do anything to try to stop me?"

"We will let nature take its course."

"I thank you for that," Clint said. He took some money out of his pocket and gave it to Hector.

As Clint was walking back to the house, he heard Hector Rio mutter, "We hope you fail."

When Clint returned to the house Sally had just come from making certain that both her father and her guest were comfortable.

"Coffee?" she offered.

"Sounds good," Clint said, and went into the kitchen with her.

They sat at the table, each with a cup.

"Tell me who it is, Clint," she said.

"You'd better get some sleep," he told her. "You can use the couch."

"It's Lujan, isn't it? God, with the spread he's got, you'd think he'd be satisfied." When Clint didn't reply she said, "It is José, isn't it? It can't be Will Mills. He's Pa's friend."

"Sally, I'm not sure who it is."

"But you think you know."

"I'll know for sure once I corner Bogart."

"And what if he corners you first?" she asked. "Take some of the men with you."

"No," Clint said.

"Why not?"

"Because they're loyal to you and your father. I'm not going to ask them to stand with me against a gun like Ray Bogart. I won't have their blood on my hands," he said. "It's bad enough Mary almost got killed."

"She offered to help," Sally reminded him. "Don't go feeling guilty about that."

"Besides," he went on, "I shouldn't need any help against Bogart."

"Can you beat him?"

He looked into Sally's eyes, saw the concern there and said, "Of course I can beat him."

"Are you always so sure, Clint?" she asked. "Have you always been sure that you were the fastest?"

"I don't think about it. Now, go and get some sleep."

"What are you going to do?"

"Make plans," he said, "and drink some more of your delicious coffee."

"You are a sweet-talking man, Clint Adams," she said, standing up. "I only wish it was more than my coffee that you wanted."

"Go to bed, lady."

She made a face at him, and he could see the strain of the day showing on her.

Soon, he thought, the strain will be over for everyone.

TWENTY-SIX

In the morning Clint waited for Andrew Fountain to wake up before he left.

"I think I have it figured out," he told the old man, "but I want you to let me put an end to this my way."

"As long as you finish it once and for all."

"No matter who's involved?"

"No matter who."

"All right, then," Clint said, and left the old man's room.

Sally and Mary were waiting in the parlor, both looking rested, fresh-faced, pretty—and worried.

"You two stay here until I get back," he instructed in a tone that said he would stand no arguments.

It didn't do him any good because they both started arguing at the same time.

"Quiet!" he bellowed, and they both fell silent. "I don't want to have to worry about anything but my neck today. If I have anything else on my mind I could get killed. Understand?"

"Yes," Mary said.

It took Sally a little longer but she finally relented.

First he rode to the Slash-J to talk to José Lujan.

"You've been very cooperative so far," Clint told Lujan. "I need your help now."

"I want this thing to end so I can get back to my business, Clint," Lujan said. "Tell me what you want me to do."

"I don't want any of your men to leave the ranch today," Clint said.

"Why?"

"If one man was bought, there could be others. I don't want to have to worry about how many guns I'm going up against."

Lujan thought a moment, then said, "Very well. I take it you know who the guilty one of us is."

"Yes."

"Who?"

"You'll find out when it's all over," Clint said. "Just make sure you know where all your men are."

"I know who the loyal ones are," Lujan assured him, "and they will watch the others."

"Thanks."

"*De nada*," Lujan said as Clint mounted Duke. "*Vaya con Dios.*"

As Clint Adams rode into town Ray Bogart's employer watched from the window of his office.

"He's here," William Mills said. He turned from his window and looked at the man seated across from him, the man he'd hired to kill his partners and the Gunsmith.

"It's about time," Bogart said.

"You'll have to do it today and then leave town," Mills said. "The sheriff is still looking for who killed Sam Wager last night."

"I told you I didn't have any choice."

"Yes," William Mills said, "you told me."

Well, at least Bogart had forced the issue. By killing Wager, he'd narrowed Adams' search down to him.

"I guess it's time to end it," he said, without realizing that he had spoken aloud.

"Oh, I'll end it, all right—" Bogart said, uncrossing his legs and standing up, "with a bang."

"Just kill him," Mills said, "and then ride. Is your horse out back?"

"Ready and waiting."

"Good."

Mills turned his back to look out the window again, and heard the door to his office open and then close firmly behind him.

Bogart stood for a moment outside the door of

William Mills and took a deep breath. His lungs were tingling, as was his right hand. It was finally going to happen.

The death of a legend—and the birth of one.

Mills had done what he had done out of blind panic. Looking at Andrew Fountain had frightened him, because soon he would be as frail as "old" Andrew, who was scarcely six years his senior.

He was on the verge of becoming an old man, and what had he accomplished? He had no wife, and he knew better than to hope that Sally would ever become that. Still, he had hoped that she would at least try his bed, as she had tried the bed of many others in town, but soon even that became a forlorn hope.

It had been relatively easy to have somebody pass a rumor to Ben Williams that he was being cheated out of his fair share of his profits from the Salt Ring. Cheated by all of his partners, and especially by Andrew Fountain, who was its unofficial leader.

As Fountain's friend, Mills had known that he was becoming increasingly agitated by Ben Williams's complaints, and that sooner or later Andrew Fountain would blow up.

He had hoped that one would kill the other, and in his panic had not cared who died, but things had worked out even better. Both Williams and Jud Clark had been killed and for a while it looked like even Fountain might pass on, but his injuries had not proved fatal enough for that.

Still, it had begun, and then Clint Adams had arrived, exactly on the day that his plan began to go into effect.

Ray Bogart was supposed to be the remedy for the Gunsmith's interference, but Mills had soon found other uses for him.

Things did not go smoothly, however. He had hoped that one of the remaining partners—Fountain, Lujan, or especially Sam Wager—would crack under the strain and somehow indict themselves, but surprisingly enough cooler heads prevailed. Clint Adams appeared to be having that effect on Lujan and Fountain. When Wager had called for the meeting, Mills had hopes of inciting something, but again Clint Adams was present, taking control away from him.

And now, with the unplanned death of Wager the situation had been forced and Mills was not sorry.

At least it would end now, one way or another.

TWENTY-SEVEN

Clint left Duke at the livery and then walked back down El Paso Street. The Whiskey River Saloon was shut tight, not only closed but boarded up, probably because of Sam Wager's death.

El Paso Street was strangely deserted, even for that hour of the morning. It was as if the people in the town knew what was coming and wanted to be out of harm's way.

Clint continued past the Whiskey River toward William Mills's office, and caught sight of Mills looking out of his window. Good, the man knew he was coming for him.

Clint knew, however, that before he could get to Mills he would have to go through Ray Bogart.

Bogart had left Mills's office and waited in an alley across the way. From there he was able to watch the length of El Paso Street as it extended towards the livery stable. That was the way Clint

Adams would come, he was sure. They both knew that this meeting had to take place in the middle of the street.

Sally Fountain and Mary Randall had decided that they couldn't stay away, so they saddled two horses and rode towards town, hoping to get there in time. They knew there was no way they could stop what was going to happen, but neither woman was prepared to simply stay behind and wait for the outcome.

They wanted to see it.

Clint spotted Bogart immediately as the man stepped out of an alley across from Mills's office. They walked toward each other and stopped when they were close enough to hear each other without shouting.

"Adams."

"Bogart."

"That's right," Bogart said.

"The man who likes to beat women."

Bogart smiled at that, recognizing it as a ploy to try and upset him.

"You won't make me mad, Adams, and I won't get careless," he said. "I've been waiting for an opportunity like this for a long time."

"An opportunity to die?" Clint asked. "That's a hell of a thing to spend a lifetime waiting for."

"But I don't figure my time is here yet," Bogart said, smiling.

"It won't be," Clint said, "if you'll turn around and ride out of here."

Bogart shook his head.

"I can't do that," he replied. "I've got a job to do and I'm getting paid good money to do it."

"No amount of money is worth dying for, Bogart."

"I'm through talking," Bogart said. His right hand moved swiftly and surely toward his gun.

And the Gunsmith made his move.

Bogart's gun was almost out of his holster when the bullet struck him in the chest. He blinked rapidly, puzzled, wondering what had hit him. He couldn't feel anything and thought that maybe he'd imagined it. His vision was clear, and he saw that the Gunsmith's gun was out. He looked down at his right hand and saw that it had opened and his gun was on the ground. He bent over to pick it up, but keeled over face-first in the dirt.

When the bullet struck Bogart in the chest William Mills flinched, imagining that he could feel the gunman's pain. The lawyer turned away from his window, seated himself at his desk, and opened the top drawer. Adams would be coming for him now, but that wouldn't be for a few moments yet—time enough for him to do what he had to do.

He only hoped that he would have the courage to do it.

Mary and Sally came riding up El Paso Street

just as Bogart fell. They hurried toward Clint as he knelt down next to the body.

"Is he dead?" Sally asked as they reached him.

He looked up at them, frowned and demanded, "What the hell are you two doing here?"

"We had to come, Clint," Mary said. "Don't be angry."

"I've just killed a man, and you ask me not to be angry?" he said.

"But he was trying to kill you," Sally said.

"That doesn't make any difference," Clint said. "No difference at all."

He kicked Bogart's gun and sent it spinning through the dust until it came to rest against the boardwalk across the street.

"What now?" Sally asked.

"Now I'm going to visit a lawyer."

"Oh, no," Sally said, shaking her head sadly. William Mills had always been her father's friend.

"Come on," Clint said, "before that fool sheriff comes running out."

They crossed the street towards Mills's office. They were climbing the steps to the second floor when they heard the report of a single shot.

"What was that?"

"That," Clint Adams said, "was the sound of a lawyer playing judge and jury."

TWENTY-EIGHT

Unfortunately, the cleanup involved talking to Sheriff Biegelheisen.

By the time the bodies of Bogart and Mills had been moved to the undertaker's office, both José Lujan and Andrew Fountain had arrived in town. Like Sally Fountain and Mary Randall, both men had become impatient with waiting for word of the outcome and decided to ride to town to find out for themselves.

They were all crowded into the small sheriff's office. Biegelheisen was trying to get to the root of the matter in his own abrasive, incompetent way.

"I don't understand why I wasn't informed about what was going on," he complained.

"It didn't seem advisable, Sheriff," Clint Adams replied.

"Why the hell not?" the man demanded. "I'm the sheriff here."

"That's true, but all I had were suspicions—"

"What about after this young woman was beaten up? Why wasn't I notified then?"

"She, uh, didn't want to press charges," Clint explained.

The sheriff looked at Mary and she nodded.

"I still don't understand," the little lawman whined. "You claim that William Mills was responsible for the murder of four of the most important men in this town? And that he just shot himself?"

"That's the way it is or was, Sheriff," Andrew Fountain said, and José Lujan nodded his agreement.

"No, sir," the sheriff said, "I don't think I can just accept your word for what went on. I'm going to have to investigate—"

"That's too bad, Sheriff," Fountain said, interrupting him, "because Mr. Adams here has to leave town almost immediately."

Clint looked at Sally and Mary and said, "Tomorrow, at the latest."

"You can't do that," the sheriff said. "I have to investigate. You have to stay in El Paso until I've completed my—"

"He's leaving, Sheriff," Fountain said, wondering more than ever what had ever possessed them to appoint him sheriff. Still, they appointed him, they could damn well unappoint him.

"I say when he leaves," the little man sputtered, "because I'm the sheriff!"

"That," Andrew Fountain said firmly, tired of hearing the man repeat that statement, "can be fixed!"

After they left the sheriff's office, Sally told Clint to come over to Mary's room in the saloon when he was finished talking with Andrew Fountain and José Lujan.

"It's boarded up, isn't it?"

"The back door will be open," Sally told him. "Just come up to her room. We want to show you something."

She left, and Clint walked her father back to his buckboard, accompanied by José Lujan.

"Well, I guess you two are what's left of the El Paso Salt Ring," Clint said. "What do you plan to do?"

"Well," Fountain said, settling himself down on the seat of the buckboard, "I think we'll have to talk about it, but knowing José as I do, I suspect we'll just get back to business as usual."

He looked at José, who nodded and said, "And I might add, it is about time."

"Business as usual?" Clint asked in disbelief. "After all the trouble you've been through? Why not make the salt beds free again so other people can make a living out of it."

"Clint," Andrew Fountain said, "we appreciate everything you've done, but please, when it comes to business—mind your own?"

Clint watched Andrew Fountain ride off.

"I can't believe this. I suppose you two will take

on new partners as well," Clint said to Lujan.

"It would make sense."

"José, you're an intelligent man—"

"—which is why I want to get back to my business," Lujan interrupted. "Adios, my friend."

Lujan mounted up, and Clint watched him ride out of town, shaking his head and wondering about men who didn't learn from their mistakes.

TWENTY-NINE

He found the back door of the Whiskey River Saloon open as promised and took the back stairs to the second floor. The door to Mary's room was closed, but when he knocked she called out, "It's not locked."

He walked in, and was greeted by a sight that made him forget his exasperation at the Salt Ring.

Mary and Sally were on the bed, smiling broadly and wearing nothing at all. The contrast between the very different bodies of the two women was striking and somehow erotic.

"So this is what you wanted to show me," he asked huskily.

"This," they said together, jumping off the bed, "and more!"

They moved in on Clint and began to undress him, one starting on his shirt and the other on his pants. He could feel the heat from their naked bodies as they pressed against him.

When they had him as naked as they were they each took a hand and tugged him onto the bed, settling Clint in between them.

Obviously, they had planned this, because they knew exactly what to do next. Sally got down between his legs and began to lick his hardened shaft, while Mary leaned over him and dangled her hard little tits in his face. He took them in his mouth alternately while Sally sucked on him. Then Sally said, "Now, Mary."

Sally straddled his hips so that the tip of his swollen cock was prodding the moist lips of her pussy, and Mary eased her way up until her mound was virtually in his face. Clint could no longer see Sally, but he felt her as she suddenly sat on his cock, taking it all the way inside of her hot tunnel. He began to lap at Mary eagerly while Sally rode him hard.

He reached around to cup Mary's firm ass and pull her closer to him so that he could thrust his tongue deeper inside her. As he felt Sally working him towards a massive orgasm, he found Mary's clit and began to suck on it.

Their mutual climax was like an earthquake. Sally cried out as he began to shoot inside of her, and Mary screamed and ground her crotch into his face as she was wracked by spasms of pleasure.

"You girls worked this out, didn't you?" he asked them while they all rested.

"Oh, yes. We agreed that this was the way we should say our good-byes to you," Mary said.

"And it's a good-bye I'll always remember," he said fervently.

The girls began to laugh and exchange glances. "It's not over yet," Mary said.

"It's not—" he started to say, but Mary's head was suddenly between his legs, and he could feel her tongue working up and down his semi-erect shaft.

"Sally—" he said, but she silenced him by pressing her nipples against his face. He gave in and began to lick and suck her.

The plan was the same, only they changed positions. When Mary had him fully erect she gave the word and hopped on him, burying his joint in her hot cunt to the hilt. Sally sat on his chest and slid her vagina over his chest hair until it was right in front of his face, ready for his tongue.

He pulled her close, as he had done to Mary, and began to tongue her avidly while moving his hips in time to the motion of Mary's powerful thighs. The earth seemed to shake once again as they all shouted in ecstasy.

There was definitely something to be said for long good-byes.

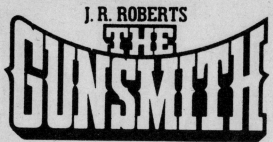

J. R. ROBERTS
THE GUNSMITH

SERIES

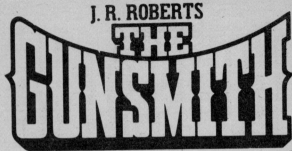

J. R. ROBERTS
THE GUNSMITH

SERIES